HUGH MACDONALD

AND ALL THE STARS SHALL FALL

THE LAST WILD BOY, BOOK 2

THE ACORN PRESS
CHARLOTTETOWN
2017

Praise for *Chung Lee Loves Lobsters:*

"This timeless tale by PEI's Poet Laureate has long been a favourite in PEI, winning the L. M. Montgomery Children's Literature Award when it was originally published. Now, almost 20 years later, it has been has been updated with new illustrations and a revised text and released for a new generation of children to enjoy."

- Canadian Materials

Praise for *The Last Wild Boy:*

"This novel reminds me of Lois Lowry's *The Giver,* Margaret Atwood's *The Handmaid's Tale* and, peripherally, *Bumped* by Megan McCafferty. It has echoes of the style of *Among The Hidden* by Margaret Peterson Haddix and Jeanne DePrau's *The City of Ember* as well, and is a new, thought-provoking novel for YA readers from Canadian poet Hugh MacDonald."

- Tantina Davis, *Turning Pages*

"Hugh MacDonald, poet laureate of Prince Edward Island, has applied his craft and created an elegant concept novel that deals with issues of constructed gender and sexual identities."

- Canadian Materials

"Best Book for Kids and Teens pick"

- Canadian Children's Book Centre

ACORNPRESS
P.O. Box 22024
Charlottetown, Prince Edward Island
C1A 9J2
acornpresscanada.com

Printed in Canada by Marquis
Edited by Penelope Jackson
Cover design and interior layout by Matt Reid

Library and Archives Canada Cataloguing in Publication

MacDonald, Hugh, 1945-, author
And all the stars shall fall / Hugh MacDonald.

Sequel to: Last wild boy.
Issued in print and electronic formats.
ISBN 978-1-927502-97-6 (softcover).--ISBN 978-1-927502-98-3 (HTML)

I. Title.

PS8575.D6306A82 2017 jC813'.54 C2017-906695-1
C2017-906696-X

Canada

Canada Council for the Arts Conseil des Arts du Canada

The publisher acknowledges the support of the Government of Canada, The Canada Council for the Arts Block Grant Program and the Province Of Prince Edward Island.

I would like to dedicate this book
to the planet earth and all who strive to save it
and to live in peace and justice upon it.

Part I

Chapter 1: Aahimsa Under Attack

The general alarm shattered Alice's dream and brought her suddenly upright in her bed. The dream had been pleasant, about an upcoming birthday party. In her dream she would be twelve years old in a few months. She remembered that the party had been fun and she was wearing a brand new dress. It was blue to match her pretty eyes — like her mother's, only lighter.

She sat there in bed, her dream shattered, feeling stunned and frightened, wearing a frilled, ivory cotton nightdress, and rubbing her sleepy blue eyes. Her long blond hair, though tousled and in disarray, made a halo around her lovely, almost twenty-eight-year-old face. Sometimes she wished she were still almost twelve, like her daughter, Tish. Life had been so much simpler back then.

Blanchfleur, Alice's mother, stood in the doorway of her daughter's bedroom, her tired, round face ashen in the sudden electric brightness. It was obvious to the daughter that her mother, the mayor, had taken no trouble to fix her full head of blond hair or to apply makeup. Her usually attractive face looked drawn and angry.

My daughter, the independent young mother, thought the agitated mayor, *still looks like a frightened little girl sometimes.*

"Turn off those damned lights, Mother," Alice snapped. The fiery blue rings within her almond eyes still burned with a nagging resentment toward her mother that hadn't completely eased since the day the mayor almost murdered Alice's once-beloved companion, Nora, intentionally and in cold blood.

"No time. Get up and come with me now. It may already be too late to save the City of Aahimsa," said Mayor Blanchfleur. "Not to mention Tish, and ourselves."

Alice rose up on her elbow, about to answer, but her mother had already left the room. Alice scrambled to her feet, wrapped herself in her plush housecoat, stepped into furry, ivory-tinted slippers, and hurried down the hall with rapidly beating heart. The fierce, unrelenting scream of the emergency alarm had begun to drill itself into her consciousness and already had upset her stomach. What was going on? She had never heard this particular deafening alarm before.

She found her mother seated in the same dimly lit control room where the two had struggled and even tried to injure one another a few short years before. Blanchfleur, dressed in yesterday's rumpled grey suit, sat rigidly upright in her tired old chair and stared open-mouthed at the flickering screen.

"Could you turn off that alarm?" Alice growled, then moved up close enough to the screen to read the message that was printed there in bold script.

"I can't," Blanchfleur said, her voice unable to cover up her despair and near panic. Alice had never seen her mother like this. "I tried several times and I don't seem to have control of the system anymore. The message on the screen was already here when I arrived. It must have come before we lost contact with the Manuhome."

The Manufacturing Homeland had always been her mother's passion. The vast agricultural and manufacturing centre, well outside the walls of Aahimsa, had brought great wealth to the city from its sales throughout the feminized city-states of the world. It was operated by the world's last outsiders — slaves, in Alice's opinion — who had had the bad luck to be born male.

Alice turned her attention back to the screen. It held a simple, curt text message: *Minutes ago received urgent message from Agrihome exterior: deadly night spray action conducted by drones across entire Agrihome area, everyone on the outside dead or dying. Get your family underground and hide. We're on our way down to the escape tunnels. Best of luck. U*

"It's from Ueland." The mayor turned to Alice, who was still barely awake. "Get yourself and the child dressed quickly and grab a few necessities for you both." Blanchfleur stepped to the window. There was unusual, frantic movement in the sky outside, like flocks of birds gone wild. Somehow the protective dome wasn't functioning. Numerous drones flitted about, cute little things if they weren't so deadly, some of them a bit too close to them. In the near distance a blinding flash, and they watched as the Palace of the Temple Donors disappeared in a brilliant ball of light. The Manor House that served as Council Headquarters for the City of Aahimsa as well as the Mayor's Residence shook violently.

"Great Goddess," said Alice, clinging to her mother's arm. "Can't you do something?"

"This is what we feared," said Blanchfleur. "Get Tish up out of bed as is and let's get quickly underground. Never mind your things. Hurry! Meet me at the elevator." As she finished speaking, all the electric lights went to black and the nearest window shattered, spraying shards of glass that rolled like waves of blood around the room as red emergency lights popped on overhead. "Go," she snapped, pushing Alice outside, then slamming the heavy steel door and locking it. "Get Tish and nothing else. Hurry!" Her voice now left no room for argument as it rose to shrill panic.

The elevator in the nearby hall took them rapidly down, the three generations of females: Mayor Blanchfleur in her rumpled suit, Alice wrapped in her baby-blue housecoat, and Tish in pink flannel pyjamas and matching cotton wrap. The only concession to their comfort and safety were the three pairs of shoes they had put on to replace their slippers. Eleven-year-old Tish carried a small suitcase containing all of her fashion dolls.

When the elevator reached the basement level, Blanchfleur removed her normal skeleton key and inserted a second one, this with a longer tongue. Alice had never seen it before. No sooner had her mother turned it clockwise than the car began to shudder and shake. Blanchfleur pushed several of the buttons and the elevator began its rapid descent again, and after a minute or so lurched to a sudden stop. The mayor removed her key and pocketed it as the door slid open, revealing an underground area of deep darkness.

"Everybody out, quickly. We have only a couple of minutes." She retrieved a small flashlight from her pocket and the two younger women followed, not wanting to remain too long in the lightless void they had entered. Blanchfleur unlocked a solid metal door and they entered a second smaller darkened room, locking the first door behind them. She stepped to the left and they heard a soft click and the room lit up. "Wait," she whispered.

Moments later they heard a muffled explosion in the distance and the earth shuddered, causing a fine rain of dust to fall from the rough ceiling overhead.

Alice was frightened, but when she saw the terror in Tish's eyes she steeled herself and managed a forced smile. She laid one arm across her daughter's shoulders and pulled her close. "What now, Mom?" she asked Blanchfleur as calmly as she could manage.

"We wait until the ground settles and then we enter Ueland's tunnel and see where it takes us."

"Ueland...he is the outsider who runs the Manuhome, isn't he?" Alice asked.

"Used to be. The Manuhome is, in all likelihood, destroyed and non-existent by now, and maybe Doctor Ueland is gone with it," said her mother. "I warned you this might happen." She saw the faces of her daughter and granddaughter wince and stiffen. "But maybe not," she said, managing a weak smile. "Let's hope. Are you prepared to travel on a real adventure?"

"I'm cold," said Tish. She was tall for her age, long-legged and blond and pretty like her mother. She was also an intelligent child, strong and determined. She would certainly need strength and determination as well as brains in the days ahead, her grandmother thought.

Blanchfleur smiled at Tish. "Yes, it's cold down here. But there's no time to worry about little things like the temperature. This isn't going to be easy, but let's show Grandmother we can do it. Let's get going while we still can."

"I'd rather go back up to our house," said Tish. Alice looked from her daughter to her mother.

"We can't," said Blanchfleur. "That explosion you heard destroyed the shaft. The elevator won't go up; it won't go anywhere. But we wouldn't want to go back anyway, because by now they've destroyed the Manor and everything in it. I'm sorry, Tish, but we're still alive and together, and for the moment, that's all that matters." Blanchfleur stepped to the door marked "EXIT TO TUNNEL. PLEASE

WATCH YOUR STEP." She pushed the door, but it wouldn't budge. She shrugged and entered her password into the small keyboard next to the door and it beeped and said "PASSWORD INVALID" on the tiny screen. She tried again and got the same result. She returned to the door through which they'd entered the room and it wouldn't budge. "Oh my," she said, and sat on a bench along the wall. She did her best not to panic.

"What's wrong, Grandma?" asked Tish.

"I don't know, dear," she said. "Let's just give it a minute.

Alice tried one door after another and looked out through the glass panel in both into the exterior blackness. Then she began to punch the glass in frustration.

"The glass is very strong and thick. You couldn't even shoot a bullet through it," said the mayor.

"What can we do?"

"I don't know. I'm trying to remember the plan. Perhaps we were supposed to wait. It's a long time since Doctor Ueland and I discussed a situation like this as a possibility. Perhaps we are supposed to wait until someone comes. I'm not sure, but I don't know what else to do. There's one good thing, though."

"What's that, Mother?" asked Alice.

"If we can't get out, no one can get in either."

Alice lowered her voice so Tish wouldn't hear. "But what if no one comes to help?"

"That could happen, I guess. But let's hope not. Someone will come. I'm counting on it."

As Blanchfleur finished speaking, Alice hugged her mother, and Tish, who was becoming more and more alarmed, moved close beside them, observing the looks of desperation on both of their faces.

Then a huge tremor shook the floor under their feet, the result of the most recent distant but violent explosion. Blanchfleur, though she knew it had been a massive blast, attempted to send her daughter and granddaughter a comforting look just as all the lights blacked out, leaving them in total darkness.

Chapter 2: Ueland Saves Adam

Doctor Ueland hadn't been able to sleep. He'd lain in bed, his thin face grim, his small dark eyes darting about the walls of his room, following the racing shadows of fast-moving clouds the full moon had been painting across his walls, his lean body clamped tight with tension and stress. He'd received reports from several of his best workers of a marked increase in the number of surveillance drones dipping and swooping around the various parts of the Manuhome over the past few days.

He had suspected that something bad was in the offing, his first guess being that the global authorities had been searching for any signs they could find of Adam, the bright young boy who had been raised among the old ones at Happy Valley in the wild outside Aahimsa. The long-rumoured wild boy who Mabon, the former Ranger, and Nora, former companion to Blanchfleur's daughter, Alice, had risked everything to save and to raise lovingly as their own child. The same wild boy Ueland had been harbouring in the Manuhome these almost three years.

Ueland wondered if the two runaway lovers who had raised the boy as their own had been killed, or if they were still on the run, hiding from the insiders. He hoped Nora and Mabon had escaped the Forest Rangers, the powerful and violent outsider police force in the wild. The Rangers did whatever the controllers in Aahimsa ordered them to do. They lived every moment having their every word and every angry thought monitored by the controllers. Each of them carried a device buried under the skin at the base of their necks that not only spied on them, but also could be exploded by the controllers at any instant.

The boy, Adam, would certainly be happy and relieved if his adoptive parents had managed to escape capture.

Ueland had just begun to doze when the Manuhome alarms had started going off all around him and he'd begun to receive a series of frantic calls from his various managers, and suddenly there was no more time for wondering.

When those scattered reports started arriving from all across the Agrihome only minutes before, reports of flares and bright explosions lighting up the Agrihome and blasting everything apart, of fields drenched with toxins and luscious greenery turned almost instantly black, of the windows of all its buildings and residences shattered by violent explosions, of broken bodies of scattered, dead, and dying outsider labourers: some smothered in their beds by the toxins, others fallen wherever they may have been standing in the residences, or while trying to flee on the outside; some few still living but aware of death's inevitability even as they spoke to the doctor who had, at once, sent off a brief warning message to Blanchfleur in her Manor House in Aahimsa.

Most callers had warned him to get away at once, as there was no escaping the odourless gas, or whatever it was. He knew this horror wasn't Blanchfleur's doing; she would never do anything like this. She was capable of ordering horrible actions when necessary, but she, too, was fighting for her life and for her principles. The Manuhome and its workers were a vital part of that fight.

So Ueland reasoned that if the mayor's beloved workers were a target, then she and her family were also slated for death, and with them the end of everything he and Blanchfleur had been hoping to accomplish.

Shortly after sending the note, the whole of Aahimsa's communications system had been shut down. He was surprised. Someone in the Manuhome must be betraying him — poor fool, he would be killed with all of the others. Ueland wondered if Blanchfleur had even received the message. He hoped so. He knew what he had to do. The emergency procedures he and Blanchfleur had agreed on should they ever come under attack from outside would have to be followed. He would know soon enough if she had received the message.

Now he was using his key to open the boy's door. Adam always locked it when he was inside by himself. He was a fine eleven-year-old lad, nearly twelve, an obedient boy. Ueland had knocked several times. But the boy was a very deep sleeper who had trained himself to wake to his alarm. He rarely heard a knocking on his thick door. The doctor was forced to use his skeleton key.

Ueland opened the door silently and stepped inside the darkened, windowless room. He moved past the open door, and suddenly he was knocked to the floor by the wiry boy, who assumed he was fighting for his life against an unknown intruder in the pitch black. Adam was on him, holding a butcher's knife against his throat, his fierce dark-brown eyes burning in the room like those of an angry, wild dog.

"Adam," he gasped, "don't cut, it's me, Ueland."

"Sorry," the boy mumbled, fighting his way out of his trance-like fury.

"'S okay," said Ueland, getting to his feet and rolling his head around, trying to ease the stiffness and to compose himself. He had to be sharp and decisive. Their time to flee was likely almost up. Whatever was killing his workers would soon be upon them also. "We have to run. Come now, leave everything. It's the World Council. They are ending everything. I have all the gear we need below. I've ordered the evacuation of the Manuhome. It will not help everyone, but there's nothing else we can do. Let's get below."

Adam knew what the doctor meant. He knew about the

elevator that led to the level below, and the narrow staircase that went farther down to where the ceramic heat pipes disappeared deep into the earth, extracting thermal energy from the fiery depths. He also knew that this is where the tunnels were found, the tunnels and the tracks that carried manufactured goods and agricultural products to Aahimsa and to the great waters called Ontario. It was from there that all of the city's electric power and heat were delivered through heavy cables, pipes, and tubes to the homes and businesses, to the streets and parks and even to the electronic moat that protected the city from any and all intruders, animal or otherwise. Adam's thoughts were interrupted by the loud beep indicating that they had reached the basement and Ueland had opened the door into the subterranean corridor.

"Let's go," said Ueland, who ran ahead in his blue silk pyjamas and red slippers. Adam almost laughed to see him out of his apartment without one of his many fine tailored suits and shiny black leather shoes.

After a couple of minutes, Ueland unlocked the door to the private administrative stairway they had come to on their right and they ran downstairs. When the doctor opened the door to the sub-basement, Adam was hit by waves of intense heat generated by the ceramic lined insulated heating pipes and heard the shouting voices coming from off to their left. "What's going on?" he asked.

"We're trying to evacuate as many of the surviving workers from the Manuhome as we can. The vast majority of the Agrihome workers are likely dead by now. It's too late to help them. I've vastly underrated the determination of the World Council to get rid of us all. Our Manuhome labourers are loading themselves onto cars that will take them far to the north. I've been building the escape tunnels and planning for this for some time, though I never thought it would happen this soon," said Doctor Ueland, who was now leading Adam toward another unfamiliar door along the side of the corridor.

"I never figured on them destroying the Agrihome first. They never had a chance, my poor farmer lads," the doctor said, his eyes damp and his voice cracking.

Adam had never heard Ueland like this. He hadn't seen the man express himself with such feeling on any matter. He watched anxiously as the doctor unlocked the door and they went in.

"Are we going with the workers?" asked Adam, his face hot and red from exertion and the heat of the confined, underground space. He watched impatiently as Ueland opened a closet door and was quick to help out as the older man began pulling out bundles of clothing and sleeping rolls for both of them and a large suitcase decorated with white flowers.

Adam set down the clothing bundles and took the suitcase.

"Holy," he said. "This case is heavy. What's in it, anyway?"

"Take the small bundle and get dressed. Quickly now." Ueland turned his back and removed his pyjama top. Adam did likewise and dressed quickly, feeling embarrassed, although he knew the doctor had regularly thoroughly examined him for medical reasons. But it felt different somehow outside the medical office.

"To answer your questions, we are leaving just like the workers, but not just yet. We have something important to do first. A sort of rescue," said the doctor.

"A rescue?" asked Adam, his eyes bright with curiosity.

"We are off to rescue some damsels in distress," Ueland said, smiling mischievously.

"Damsels? What are damsels?" Adam asked, wondering if the doctor was teasing him.

"I was told that you and your mother, Nora, were both avid readers."

"We were both good readers. We loved reading books and I still love to read," he said. "Who told you that?"

"Several of the old ones mentioned all the books you were devouring more than once." He paused. "I'm surprised you don't know the word *damsel*. A damsel is a helpless female," said Doctor Ueland, his eyes twinkling.

Adam was dumbstruck, as he had never heard of a helpless female. He had no idea what to expect next from Doctor Ueland. "Who are these damsels?" he asked.

"Are you ready to go?" the doctor asked, picking up the big suitcase.

"What's in that suitcase? It's so heavy," asked Adam, as he hurried to catch up.

"Lots of things. One of them is very important. There's a smaller metal case inside the large one. We mustn't ever lose that inside one. No matter what happens." He stopped a moment and looked at Adam, his face concerned. "You understand?"

"Sure. What's in it, anyway?" Adam said, serious and filled with curiosity.

"Not now, Adam. There isn't time. Are you ready?"

"I understand and I'm ready. Where are we going?"

"You'll see," said the doctor. "You may be surprised. Whatever happens, you must trust me; it will be for the best."

They opened another mysterious locked door, the next one they came to, and quickly descended yet another stairway to the next level, where they found a good-sized electric railcar sitting at a siding. The car was brightly painted and elegantly made. They climbed on board and entered a compartment that was done up with plush furnishings and equipment. It was a car fit for the kings and queens of old, the rich ones from the old history books. Adam set down the bedding he was carrying and sat on one of the comfortable padded armchairs.

"Those seats are not intended for us. Come on. You'll like these practical ones up ahead far better."

Ueland took the large suitcase and led Adam, arms full of the sleeping rolls, through a metal door with a thick black window into the forward compartment that was obviously where the driver of the railcar would sit with his helper. "Put your things on the shelf at the back and sit down," Ueland said, pointing to the chair on his left. Adam sat.

Ueland took the seat to Adam's right, in front of an instrument panel and a set of hand controls. He pulled his wallet from an inside pocket and extracted a small brass key. He inserted the key into a slot and turned it so the electric engine hummed into life and ran quietly and smoothly. He pulled back a metal lever and the railcar headed away from the siding and switched smoothly onto one of the main tracks.

Adam was suddenly excited and full of questions, which he kept to himself at first. What was going on? Then he saw an arrow on a rail-side sign pointed in the direction they were headed. It read in large bold letters: "AAHIMSA CITY CENTRE." He looked toward Ueland and asked the first question, the one he wanted answered most. "Will we be saving Nora and Mabon and Lucky? And are we safe going inside the city walls, where I was born and my mother Nora escaped to save my life? Males are forbidden to enter there."

Ueland was startled by the first question and hesitated, although he quickly realized they were obvious questions for Adam to ask. Ueland was about to answer when the earth shuddered and the railcar shook violently as an enormous explosion occurred far behind them. Ueland turned instantly back to the controls and pulled the handle close to them. Adam held on for dear life as their world was darkened by a huge cloud of dust and smoke. After a gut-wrenching bump and a hesitation, the railcar accelerated rapidly away in the direction of downtown Aahimsa.

Chapter 3: Nora, Mabon, and Lucky

Nora was the first to hear an explosion. She had been standing in her underclothes, brushing the water out of her drenched hair that reflected lines of dark copper in the bright moonlight. The sky was laced with drifting wisps of dark cloud.

Just as she had emerged, dripping, from the cool lake, she had witnessed a brilliant burst of light coming from somewhere inside the city walls, inside or from the direction of the Manuhome, and, only moments later felt the earth shudder, and heard the percussive *whump* of a massive explosion. Mabon, who was still swimming in the cool water of the lake with Lucky the dog paddling beside him, emerged from the waves a moment later, wondering why Nora stood gesturing frantically toward the city walls. Lucky shook the lake water from his thick black-and-tan fur, and as Mabon, her huge companion, gazed beyond Aahimsa, there came a second bright flash, followed by another, larger explosion. Mabon sped to Nora's side.

"We'd better get ourselves back out of sight," said Mabon. "I thought we'd be safe getting cleaned up just before daylight and at this distance from Aahimsa. But dawn is breaking."

"We're never safe, are we? But the clean-up and swim were worth the risk," said Nora. "I felt so much better just a minute ago." But what was happening to Aahimsa? She knew lots of people in there and even if the city was the home of her enemies, she hated thinking of the trouble the insiders might be in. The insiders hadn't always been her enemies; she had been raised and lived happily there until her teen years as a female with full privileges to live inside any of the walled cities on the planet. But on the day she and Alice, the mayor's daughter, discovered the baby crying under a tree, that all changed forever. The safety of she and Mabon and the foundling Adam, if they ever got him back, had to come ahead of Aahimsa and its residents.

She watched her man as he used his cotton shirt to dry his reddish-brown hair. His recent injuries had healed well and apart from a few prominent, angry fresh scars on his thigh, he seemed as good as new. He was still her lovely man, tall and broad-shouldered, his powerful muscles still rippling as one would have expected of a former Forest Ranger, but his soft eyes and his tender, long-fingered hands suited the loving, gentle giant she had learned he was.

When he noticed her staring at him, his generous mouth curled into a broad smile. She grinned at him in turn, her green, gold-specked eyes sparkling in the waning moonlight and lighting their hurried dash to the shelter, as she called back over her shoulder past him, to the hesitant dog, "Come on, Lucky, hurry!"

All three scurried up the sandy lakefront and disappeared through an opening in the fractured concrete basement, all that remained of a tall building long ago destroyed in the wars between the outsiders of long ago. The ruined basement jutted out from the crumpled sandbank and had served them well as a temporary shelter.

"What will we do?" Mabon asked. "Head out or wait and see? Are you worried about what the explosions inside the city might be doing to old friends of yours?"

"Of course I'm concerned. But we have to lay low for the time being. With the racket of these explosions we can't hear well enough to tell if something is moving and watching us from the air overhead. Come sit by me," she invited Mabon. But it was Lucky, his tail wagging happily, who first danced happily over to her. Mabon laughed and joined the pair. Nora ran her fingers through the old dog's thick, tri-coloured fur. "It's hard not to be concerned about what's happening. I don't wish harm on anyone and I don't want Alice and her family injured. But my life in Aahimsa is far enough in the past that, other than a few people, I find it hard to be too concerned about what happens in there. I'm too worried about Adam. I think about him every hour of the day."

"I'm sure Ueland is watching over him," said Mabon. "We had little choice but to try and save his life by placing him within the safety of the Manuhome. Life with us is just too risky."

"And I miss all the old ones who were murdered by Blanchfleur's Rangers," continued Nora. "What about you, do you miss them very much?"

"Yes, all of them, especially Adam and the old ones. My heart aches when I think of the life we all had together there in the Happy Valley with them. Right at this moment, though, we have to think about getting safely out of here before we are discovered. We'll wait a short while, but we should get on the move as soon as possible. We'll grab our things and head east past Aahimsa and along the lakeshore a few kilometres and find a secure new hiding place, and then try to stay put until it looks like the coast is clear. Maybe by tomorrow night we can get moving along the lake toward the east again," said Mabon.

"If we're going to change hiding places, we might as well keep heading north along the lake until we can head east across the river that empties into it just north of the lake. Still farther north there used to be huge bridges that went to the other side, but I think those were destroyed long ago."

"Where did you learn about river bridges?" asked Mabon.

"One of the old books the old ones had in their collection was called an atlas. It was a book full of maps that showed the old boundaries of outsider territories. I'm surprised I didn't ever show it to you."

"You probably did, but there were a lot of books and I was usually interested in other things I wanted to do in the valley. But we could use that atlas now," said Mabon.

"You still have me, and I can picture lots of those maps and how they looked. I used to dream about places we could run to, you and I and Adam. I can remember that one large map and see it in my head. I used to imagine us living in the abandoned places in the east. But I don't know distances — how long it takes to get anywhere on foot. Let's head out soon. The invaders attacking the city likely aren't looking for us at the moment. They have other things on their minds. We'll stay close to the water and keep to the shadows. If we follow the coast we will get to the river we seek. What do you think?" said Nora.

Mabon shrugged, looking into her worried eyes. "Makes sense," he said, reaching down and pulling her gently to her feet. "Let's get going. Come, Lucky. Heel! Stay close to us."

They were able to travel with relative ease along the edge of the lake for what they guessed was at least two hours before the sky began to really lighten. Nora turned back to look toward Aahimsa and was startled to discover what she first thought were dark clouds off to her right. Then it dawned on her what she was looking at. "Mabon," she said, pointing, her voice showing her alarm, "what is that over there?"

Mabon stopped suddenly and ran up beside her. "Thick, black smoke. It looks like it's coming from the Manuhome—"

"Adam, our Adam is over there!" Her face turned ashen

and a thin, muffled squeal of something between pain and frustration escaped her lips. She let drop her bags and her bow and quiver of precious arrows, and began first to walk and then to run out of the protection of the trees and brush into the open in the direction of the Manuhome. Mabon dashed to catch up, Lucky at his heels, and on arriving beside Nora, wrapped his warm, thick arms around her snugly and held her close, stopping her progress.

"We won't be any help to him if they see us and kill us," he said, still hugging her and drawing her gradually back toward the protection of the trees along the shore. She ceased struggling for the moment and walked beside him, her heart racing and her mind an overwhelming blur. Lucky trotted ahead, looking back at them every now and then. They slowed a moment while he set the remainder of his things beside the bags and the bow she had dropped moments before, and organized everything into a neat pile. "We can head back toward where the black smoke is rising, but we'll have to try to stay under cover, move slowly, and be very careful."

A series of distant, brilliant flashes came from where they knew the Manuhome ought to be, followed closely by a corresponding number of thundering explosions that caused the ground to shudder, but they could not leave their shelter yet. They were forced to keep low to the ground as a seemingly endless convoy of large helicopters roared directly over their heads after crossing the massive lake behind them. One after the other dropped rapidly down inside Aahimsa's high walls. The helicopters kept coming, engines rattling and roaring, their rotors whirring, entering the city like a giant swarm of ugly locusts. After about thirty minutes, several of them emerged from the city and headed back across the lake in the direction from which they'd originally come. Still many more of the frightening machines of war arrived in a steady, seemingly unending stream.

"What are they doing?" wondered Mabon as he lifted his head just enough to safely observe without being seen.

"I don't know," said Nora. She could make a dozen guesses but nothing that would explain these startling events.

As they spoke, two of the massive steel insects seemed headed directly for them, sweeping low to the ground, uncomfortably close to their grassy hiding place before swinging away and following roughly the same course out onto the lake as the others which left before them. Both Mabon and Nora got a good look through the tall windows of the copter doors and were startled to see that both were jammed full of the insider women, residents of the walled city.

"This is all so strange. What's going on?" asked Nora, shivering involuntarily and moving closer to Mabon for comfort.

"I'm not sure, but it looks to me like they're evacuating the city," said Mabon, looking into her eyes.

"Why do that?" she asked him.

He shrugged. Through this exchange their voices had been rising until they found themselves almost shouting. The deafening noise of the constant stream of helicopters coming and going continued for what seemed hours until Nora was thinking the whole city must have been emptied.

The distant brilliant flashes of light and heart-rending explosions from the direction where they had not long ago left Adam, and their powerlessness in these moments left Nora's heart close to bursting from hopelessness and terror. Her heart was telling her she had to get back to the Manuhome and try to find her adopted son, but for the moment there was no question that it would be suicidal to try.

As suddenly as they had begun, the huge explosions stopped, and as the daylight began to sweep away the natural darkness, the sky above the land where the Manuhome should be growing crops and manufacturing its goods was marred by smaller but equally horrid explosions, and the massive clouds of dark smoke kept rising higher into the heavens. No more helicopters were arriving and none were leaving the city. Mabon stood up slowly and looked around. Nora rose up stiffly and cautiously beside him; he wrapped his arm around her waist and pulled her close. Lucky pushed against their legs, whining quietly.

A moment later they were slammed flat on the ground once more, stunned and deafened by an enormous explosion. The walls of Aahimsa, well over three kilometres away, seemed to have turned to dust before their eyes and disappeared. Moments later a steady rain of fine, granulated particles fell out of the sky and settled on them like warm, suffocating snow. They turned their faces toward the ground and covered up with scarf and shirt tail, clamping their eyes shut, struggling to breathe. Mabon tucked Lucky's snout close to his chest. Nora wanted to weep, but tears were not possible in this dreadful dryness, and breathing enough to survive was more important for the moment.

After a while the dust stopped falling and, though their eyes ached, they found their hearing somewhat restored. It took them a long time to rid themselves of the worst of the gritty dust and still longer to take in what had happened. “Shock,” said Nora, mostly to herself.

“What?” said Mabon, as Lucky lay quiet and still near to them, his tail tucked close against his haunches.

“I think I’m in shock,” she said again. They turned a full circle. The thick, black smoke still rose in the west where the Manuhome had been located, but there was clearly no sign of the city. This was no illusion. It was gone. All gone — the city and the Manuhome. And Adam. What about Adam? Nora wept deeply and in near silence and Mabon held her warm sadness close.

Chapter 4: Strange Bedfellows

Alice was doing her best to control the festering knot in her gut and keep up the reassuring smile pasted on her face for Tish's benefit. However, she guessed that Tish was smart enough and knew her mother well enough to recognize the danger they were in. The time of waiting and pacing had been growing long and the deepening darkness swallowed them as the batteries for the red emergency light in the room dimmed to almost nothing. Tish sat, her back as straight as the near invisible walls and door, on a wooden chair. She hadn't spoken since the lights died. Blanchfleur was pacing back and forth between the two doors, every now and then trying one door or the other. None of them knew how much time had passed.

Then, without warning, the door to the train tracks opened and two darker silhouettes stepped into the dark room. Tish couldn't see them but she thought she could smell them, something wild and frightening that had found them all cornered in this dark cell.

Blanchfleur edged toward them. "Thank goodness," she said. "You are finally here."

As Alice and Tish cautiously approached the two latest arrivals, they realized that two outsiders were standing only metres away from them in this suffocatingly small room underneath the city of Aahimsa. The daughter and granddaughter of Mayor Blanchfleur were shocked that these two male outsiders had the gall to come so boldly here. They must be mad.

Adam glared at the older woman in the near dark and wondered who she was. He could just barely make out that she was tall and pleasant-looking and she stared open-mouthed at him as if he were a ghost. Her surprise turned briefly to suppressed anger.

No one spoke for a few moments. Finally, Ueland spat out a few words. "No time for hesitation or discussion. We have to put all of our negative feelings on hold and concentrate on getting out of here as quickly as possible. We can't go back over the tracks that brought us here. They've already destroyed all that. We have to head down the underground tunnels toward the shipping docks and seek some usable path out of here, or a safe place to hide for a while."

Alice spoke and Tish's horrified expression said that she completely agreed with her angry mother. "We're not about to go anywhere with outsiders!" The two insiders stood, hands on hips, their body language determined not to take part in any plan.

Blanchfleur remained remarkably silent, her face frustrated and pained.

"Who are you all?" asked Adam.

Ueland spoke sharply. "I'm sorry, Alice and Tish, but we're the only option you have. You can stay and die or you can come and have a chance to live. The city will be wiped out any moment now, just like the Manuhome was destroyed, along with most of its occupants, all annihilated. Whatever you had in the city before is gone. Live or die; that's it. Choose!"

Blanchfleur led the way quickly out the door without a word and the two outsiders followed, the young one first, then the older one. Alice and Tish hesitated one mere instant, then followed. Ueland and Adam scrambled up and into the forward cabin of the waiting rail coach and took their seats at the controls. Ueland flicked a switch on the console and a computer monitor screen on the dash lit up a soft green, showing the three insiders taking their seats in the luxury cabin at the rear. The insiders sat in silence, staring straight ahead like pretty robots. They had no idea what lay ahead of them. Of the train's passengers and crew, only Blanchfleur and Ueland had travelled these rails before. Only Ueland knew the tunnel system intimately. He had overseen the design of the entire system and his workers from the Manuhome had carried out the construction and regular maintenance ever since. The doctor settled into his seat and the railcar began to move slowly in the direction of the harbour front.

"Who are these insiders?" Adam asked Ueland, who was watching anxiously up ahead and to both sides as they glided with increasing speed along the tracks.

"Later, Adam," Ueland said. "Right now we have to concentrate. There are dangers up ahead. This could be our last few minutes together. So sit tight and be ready for anything. If all goes well, we'll get time to share our stories soon."

Ueland was very worried. When they had picked up Blanchfleur, her beautiful daughter Alice, and Alice's daughter, Tish, who was just a few months younger than Adam, they had been directly beneath Aahimsa's city centre. Now they were approaching the commercial harbour front. If they were spotted by any citizens they would be in trouble, and if they encountered any of the forces who had just wiped out the Manuhome — almost certainly the forces of the World Federation Council, which had been tightening its control over Aahimsa, the only city-state where any males were permitted to exist — they could all be terminated on sight. Leaving the tunnel and entering the aboveground harbour area was risky unless the attacking forces had already wiped out the rest of the city and departed. But then there would still be the possibility of further explosions or toxic gases and bacilli.

So Ueland's plan was to avoid the harbour and take one of the older, unused tracks that once took tours to some of the small islands of the lake or the river lying to the north and east. These rails had been usable the last time he had seen them, and he could activate the necessary power switches from inside the railcar. The destruction of the Manuhome may have knocked out the power connection, but since the car was still running and the tunnel lights and signals were powered up, there must be plenty of battery storage power remaining. The stored power was designed to provide hours of backup. And there were emergency generators at every station along the way. He was surprised, though, to find this section already operational. He wondered who had activated it and why. And he also realized that whoever they were, they could be waiting somewhere up ahead. But he and his passengers had no choice other than to forge ahead with their plan.

Adam remained at his side, silent but deep in thought, taking in everything that passed by the tall, curved windows of the control cabin as the train slowed and switched tracks and they turned to enter a poorly lit, dilapidated side tunnel to their left. As they made their way over the next several kilometres, the dark, damp, musty sides of the older, unused tunnel made him nervous, though the greater part of his anxiety still stemmed from the three insiders in the railcar.

He had asked Doctor Ueland who they were, but he was pretty sure he had guessed their names. The older woman had to be Blanchfleur, the mayor of Aahimsa. If so, she was the one who had wanted to kill him when he was a baby because he was a boy, and boy babies weren't allowed to live inside Aahimsa. The next oldest would be Alice, who was a friend of his mother, Nora. The two of them had found him in a basket under a tree when he was a baby. Nora had run away from the city with him in her arms and saved his life.

She had met Mabon in the wild and together they took him to see Ueland. The doctor had hidden them with the old ones in their valley for nine happy years. Then Blanchfleur sent the Rangers to attack the valley of the old ones. Blanchfleur and her Rangers drove them all out of the Happy Valley after killing all the old ones.

And now she and Alice and Tish, Blanchfleur's granddaughter, were back there in the car behind them, and, for some reason he couldn't understand, he and Ueland were helping these murderers escape. Adam looked at Ueland. The doctor sat there looking perfectly normal as he drove the railcar full of their enemies as quickly as possible away from the city.

"Who are those insiders sitting back there behind us?" he asked again.

"Fellow humans who need our help," Ueland said without batting an eye. But he was startled out of his cool manner a moment later when their world went suddenly black and the railcar's screaming brakes automatically locked. The underworld shook, and as a few emergency lights came on dimly, dirt, rocks and water poured down on them from overhead. The tunnel came apart and water pipes along the side ruptured, and some insider voices screamed in panic in the chamber behind them. As the light strengthened, the insider voices quieted and the women silently entered the forward cabin.

"Are you all right?" Ueland asked from the pilot's seat as another dim set of emergency lights lit the shattered tunnel up ahead of them. The windows of their car were streaked with dust and muddy water, but looking at the pile of debris around them it was clear that even if the car could get under power again, they weren't going to get anywhere in it.

The older woman shrugged. "How long will these lights last?" she asked, her eyes on Ueland. From the tone of her voice, Adam could tell she trusted the doctor's opinion and judgement.

Ueland merely raised his bushy eyebrows and shrugged. His voice was gentle and honest. "The batteries indicate that they are fully charged, so it depends on how much power we use. If we keep the lights low and don't run any of the electric engines, they could last two days or more, though I've never tested for that. Who knows, maybe even a week."

Alice spoke then. The sound reminded him of Nora's beloved voice. He felt his emotions welling up. He missed his mother so much. He wondered if she and Mabon were still alive. He wanted to ask Blanchfleur or this daughter of hers if they knew, but this wasn't the time. Blanchfleur looked as if she was in no mood for questions from the boy she had tried to murder more than once.

"Why don't we try and go back to Aahimsa?" Alice asked.

Blanchfleur and Ueland glanced at one another and Blanchfleur nodded at him, looking down at her feet. Ueland cleared his throat.

"Not possible," he said.

In the silence that followed, Blanchfleur looked up. "The tunnels have collapsed, and I'm afraid that there is nothing left to go back to. My guess is that our city is no more."

Adam was wondering what else they could do, and the girl at Alice's side seemed to be thinking the same thing. With a shaking voice on the verge of tears, Tish asked, "Are we going to die?"

Silence again, while the adults looked from one to another. Ueland spoke first. "No, Tish," he said kindly. "We are not going to die. Not for a long, long time." Tish looked from one insider's face to another, both of whom seemed uncertain whether they believed the doctor.

So her name is Tish, Adam thought. *Then she must be the daughter of Alice. She looks to be about my age.*

"What next?" Adam asked as he turned away from the girl.

All the insiders looked at him as if they were surprised he would speak to them. Blanchfleur seemed on the verge of responding, but Ueland sensed Adam's nervousness and jumped in. "I think we should lay low and show no signs that we're down here. We're perfectly safe for the moment. If there are no more explosions, we will make our way along the tracks and stop at the first service hatch we find."

"How far will we have to go?" asked Alice, holding Tish close beside her and rubbing her right hand along the girl's right shoulder. Adam thought again of Nora and the thousands of hours they had spent sitting together as she helped him with his reading and his lessons back in the valley.

"I didn't notice a sign of one, but they are set up every ten kilometres or so. Sometimes one site or the other wasn't suitable for construction and we had to go a bit short or long. We have gone over two kilometres from the wall, so there should be one within seven or eight kilometres."

"How long will the emergency lights last along the tracks?" asked Blanchfleur, her anxiety showing in her voice.

"I don't know. They are pretty dim, but part of that may be dirt on the lights themselves. I can't be certain. I expect they're running on emergency battery power, too. So probably no more than a few hours. But given some time they can be recharged."

"Then let's get going while we have light," said Blanchfleur. "We don't want to be walking too many kilometres in the pitch black. Are there any emergency torches on this car?"

"Yes, there are half a dozen, with a few extra batteries and a few emergency provisions." Ueland paused and spoke to everyone. "Well, what do you think?"

Adam watched everyone's faces. No one seemed sure about anything.

"Let's gather up everything we can and get going while we have this light."

"I don't want to go with them," said Tish, clinging tightly to her mother. "I'm afraid of outsiders."

"I'm afraid of your mother and grandmother," said Adam. "They hate me and want to hurt me. Why are we helping them, Doctor Ueland? You know what they tried to do to me and to Mabon and Nora." His heart pounded, afraid he may have gone too far. He glanced at Ueland, whose expression seemed unchanged, and then at Blanchfleur and Alice — he was now absolutely certain who they were.

Ueland tried his best to smile reassuringly at Adam, and then turned his face to Blanchfleur, who rose and turned toward the rear compartment.

"Yes, let's all go, but first let's spend ten minutes beginning to say the many things we must eventually say to one another. Come in here where we can all sit like civilized people. Come on, Doctor Ueland, bring the boy with you and I'll bring my girls. Then we can say a few things each. We can't possibly solve all our issues here and now, but we can make a small start. Who would like to go first?" There was only silence as all found seats, Adam sitting close to Ueland, Blanchfleur opposite the doctor with Alice on her right and Tish to her mother's right.

"Okay, then. I'll begin. I'll tell the truth and I hope you will do likewise. You may not believe me, but with time you'll see that I am honest, if little else. I will also say that we are on the same side. In a way, we always have been. From today forward we have no other choice. And, Adam — that is your name, isn't it?" She waited for an answer.

"Yes," he said.

"Well, Adam. You were right. I tried to have you terminated. I only wanted to save Aahimsa. I failed in that, it seems. I promise you I will only try to help you from now on. I will do everything in my power to protect each and every one of us. We have to work together to find another way to live together in peace."

"Why should I believe you?" Adam asked her, his face determined, his jaw set.

Blanchfleur turned then to Ueland. "Do you believe me, Doctor Ueland?" she asked, a smile on her round face.

"I have never known you to lie," he said, smiling back at her.

"Unlike yourself," she said, her friendly expression unchanged.

"We both did what we had to do to protect what we believed in and to protect each other," he said. "I'm sorry I had to deceive you, but you held all the cards, all the power. But yes, I believe you."

Blanchfleur turned back to Adam. "Do you believe me now?"

"Maybe." He was more and more confused. All the old rules no longer meant anything. They were headed into the unknown in more ways than one.

Alice and Tish had remained silent, but they looked to Adam as baffled and lost as he was.

Ueland turned to the girls. "Adam and I are your only friends for the moment. Remember that we saved your lives. We will do all we can to keep you safe as we travel together. You will learn many things about us and about surviving in this new world that will change the way you see the wild places we live in. And you will teach us many things we do not know. But now we have to go before the darkness makes our travelling impossible. Let's get going."

Ueland picked up his suitcase as everyone gathered up anything from the railcar that might prove useful and they made their way in silence along the battered, dark, and depressing rail bed.

Chapter 5: The End of the Manuhome

"I'm heading for the Manuhome," Nora said after they had stood motionless together a long time. Their hearing, numbed by the explosion, had begun to return a little at a time, though their heads ached and there remained a continuous ringing in their ears. They had finished brushing away the worst of the dust that coated their bodies and clothing following Aahimsa's powerful final blast.

"We have to find Adam." She began to stumble off away from Mabon, heading toward the wild and the Manuhome where they had left Adam under the protection of Doctor Ueland almost three years before.

Mabon hesitated a moment, knowing from experience that the series of blasts they had heard coming from the site of the Manuhome was very unlikely to allow for survivors at the point of impact. Then, seeing that Nora was going nowhere until she saw the damage for herself, he followed her.

They had travelled a few hundred metres before they noticed Lucky's distant barking. They turned to look back to where he still sat near the point where they had stood when the last explosion occurred.

"Come, Lucky," Mabon called and then whistled loudly.

The dog refused to budge.

"Let's go," said Mabon. "He needs time to calm down; he'll catch up eventually."

They carried on, Mabon taking the lead, his jaw set, eyes hard and cold as a winter sky, with Nora following, looking behind her at frequent intervals in search of any sign of Lucky coming with them. Eventually they crossed the nearest corner of what had been the dead zone outside Aahimsa, that dismal area cleared of all vermin or wild things that might find their way inside the walls, and Mabon recognised that they were entering the fringes of the wild in an area where he had spent all those lonely years as a disgraced Ranger demoted to a common cleaner. His punishment had been to tidy up all remains of creatures destroyed by the defenses of the city wall and its electronic devices that targeted any creature that dared to crawl or fly inside the immense stonework surrounding Aahimsa.

The other part of the punishment had been isolation: he had lived completely alone in the dark area of death and destruction in a tiny and miserable hut.

Neither he nor Nora could fully comprehend the scene before them. The vast, treed expanse of the wild that had been Nora, Mabon, and Adam's salvation just twelve years before was no longer recognizable. At that time, Adam's biological mother had fallen to her death from the wall, and Mabon sealed his fate by helping her — and by touching her, breaking insider law. During those same hours, Nora had fled the city with baby Adam, the tiny outsider she had saved because he was sentenced to death for being born outside the determination. His was not an authorized birth and so he could not live. Nora refused to accept the decision and chose to risk her own freedom and safety to save the child.

Here and there a lone tree, shorn of bark and leaves, stood like burnt bone, desolate amid the destruction, but everywhere else, mangled and twisted trees lay where they had fallen or were stacked in huge mounds as if carelessly tossed there.

"I'm going to climb up one of these piles of wreckage. We can't travel any distance across this mess. Maybe we can see across to the Manuhome from the top. I'm guessing there won't be much of anything to see anyway," Mabon said. Nora grimaced and stepped toward him. They held one another in silence for a few moments before separating.

Nora followed Mabon as they approached the closest mound, climbing and jumping, stumbling and climbing some more, then ducking under and scrambling over huge fallen trees until they stopped at the base of an enormous mountain of trees, rocks, and dirt thrown up by the destruction of Ahimsa and its Manuhome.

"I'm going up. You wait here," said Mabon, his face determined to appear as optimistic as he could manage to make it.

"I'm going, too. I need to see for myself," said Nora, eyes simmering with the heat of suppressed anger and despair, her gut holding its own mound of something that felt to her as ugly and heavy as stone.

They climbed slowly upward, helping one another when possible, their bodies scratched and bruised by needles and thorns and jagged, broken branches, their tips as sharp and often dangerous as knives, and stones of every size that had been tossed there by what must have been enormous, powerful explosions. As they neared the top they heard barking on the ground below them. They turned together and, in spite of their misery, smiled to see Lucky sitting patiently at the base of the pile. At the top, neither chose to immediately look in the direction of the Manuhome, instead waiting until both were standing safely together on somewhat firm footing.

"Ready?" asked Nora, placing her scratched and dirty hand in Mabon's.

"Ready," answered Mabon, applying gentle pressure to reassure her.

"Oh, no," said Nora at first glance, her voice thick and rattling with pure anguish.

Mabon said nothing but felt his chest grip with pain. He bit his lip. This was far worse than he'd expected.

Nora's knees buckled, and if Mabon hadn't caught her she might have tumbled down the enormous tangle of debris. He found them a secure spot where they could sit for a few minutes and gather the strength they needed to make the climb down and retrace their steps back to secure shelter. Both were now convinced there was no point in continuing on toward the Manuhome, even if it were physically practical, for nothing tangible remained of what had once been Aahimsa's vast and highly profitable manufacturing and agricultural homeland. Where the Manuhome had stood there were half a dozen deep interconnected craters. Nothing above or below ground could have survived those repeated powerful blasts — no building, no tunnel, no piece of equipment, no worker... nor any boy. They stayed motionless except for their occasional sobs, the shuddering agony of their despair. Both of their minds were overwhelmed by the realization that they would probably never see even a fragment of what was once there — nor of Doctor Ueland, his workers, or, worst of all, their beloved Adam.

Chapter 6: Where to Go Now?

Nora and Mabon sat up high on the mountain of debris feeling as broken and empty as the crater that had housed the Manuhome. They mulled over the scanty fragments of what had been their lives. As evening approached, and the numbing pressure on their minds eased somewhat, it occurred to Nora that they were sitting in a very exposed location where they might be detected by the eyes in the sky — distant satellites, the powerful cameras of Aahimsa's tower, or perhaps a passing drone or aircraft. She spoke her concerns to Mabon, who felt like he was awakening from a horrible nightmare.

"It's so quiet," he said. "Listen!"

Nora listened as she scanned the horizon. From where they sat it was possible to see far out into the freshwater sea, the great lake called Ontario. There were no ships moving on its surface. She looked toward where Aahimsa had been and she realized they wouldn't be seen by the eyes of the tower: the giant structure had been destroyed along with the city itself. There was only the sound of the light breeze as it moved in from the lake. There was nothing artificial that she could spot moving overhead across the sky. She and her cherished companion Mabon were the only living creatures she could see. The invaders who had so brutally attacked were nowhere to be seen. "The tower is gone," she said.

"Yes," he said. "Almost everything is gone."

"We have to go now or stay here all night. It will be cold," she said. "Let's go back and take shelter out of the wind down close to the lake. In the morning we can plan."

After slowly and carefully navigating their way down the heap of tangled trees, dirt, and rocks, they found Lucky waiting patiently below, lying at rest on the mangled earth. They made as much fuss over him as they could muster in their sorrow and fatigue as they began to walk separate and alone toward the lake, somehow avoiding the many obstacles strewn across their path by the recent demolition.

"Where do you want to go?" Mabon asked, his crooked smile nervous and unconvincing.

"Want?" After a minute of silence Nora shrugged. "I only want to be where you and Lucky are. Nothing else matters." She stopped moving away and drifted near enough for him to drape his left arm across her shoulders. Close together once more, they felt a small, warm easing of their pain. It was enough for now. Perhaps they could heal after all. *Perhaps*, she thought.

"We can't stay here, though. What about going south? It's warmer there, much less winter cold," said Mabon, pulling her closer. She put her arm partway around his waist. It still felt wonderful to be touched by her. Whatever happened to Adam, Mabon needed to carry on, to be with this woman as long as he could. But he found himself still clinging to a niggling belief that by some miracle their boy might be alive somewhere, though he could not imagine how such a miracle could ever happen. Then again, the boy had been a miracle from the beginning. He had survived the determination in Aahimsa. He had been found by Nora. Somehow he always survived; somehow all three of them had always managed to carry on.

Lucky seemed to have been infected by Nora and Mabon's deep despair and he lagged behind them, head down, occasionally whining softly. Mabon stopped every so often and rubbed the dog's large floppy ears.

"Yes," Nora said, finally responding to his remark. "But there are more large cities to the south, cities full of angry insiders, constant danger. I would rather head to the northeast."

"The northeast. Ueland says there is nothing much there anymore," Mabon said, wondering if she realized how hard life would be in that wildest of wild places.

"It is called the abandoned east," she said. "There are no cities. It is a true wild place." She remembered how, long ago, Mabon had convinced her to share his love of the wild places, and how he and Adam had travelled all around the wild outside Happy Valley with Aesop and a few others. "No one will think to look for us there."

"Don't you think they have stopped looking for us already?" he said, hopefully.

She shook her head and sighed. "No, they may never stop completely. But perhaps if we can get far enough away from here we'll better our chances of survival. The abandoned east is a cold, hard place for part of the year, but many people lived there for a long time. Many thousands of people once lived happy lives there."

"How do you know all this?" he asked.

"Those books Adam and I borrowed from Brin in Happy Valley. Also, Aesop and Brin and the other old ones spoke of how things used to be before the Insider Revolution, before the feminine era. Those books told about the settlement and long history of those places. People lived there and raised their families close to the land and sea in happiness, until cities lured them away."

By the time Nora and Mabon and the dog Lucky reached the shoreline, the moon was full in the sky off to the southeast, and they picked up the few items they had left behind when they raced toward the Manuhome after the mighty explosions there. They fed Lucky bits of smoked meat from one of their bags but agreed they wanted nothing to eat themselves. After gathering their gear and arranging a rough shelter, they lay awake, clinging together, looking out over the grey lake.

Part 2

Chapter 7: Up Along the Murky Tunnel

Adam would never understand any of this. Especially how Doctor Ueland seemed willing to forget the horrible crimes Mayor Blanchfleur had committed against him and Mabon and Nora, and especially against Brin and Aesop and the old ones in the valley.

They had left the railcar far behind and were making their way in near darkness up along the damp and chilly rail bed. At first he and Ueland had kept close together. The doctor had insisted on checking the outside third rail on their right for electric power. “Be careful,” he had warned everyone. “Adam and I are going first. We’ll make sure the high-tension rail is without electricity. That way no one will be electrocuted.”

“How far are we going today?” Adam asked Ueland.

“Not sure,” the doctor said as he took long strides on his wiry, muscular legs. Adam had never seen him move so fast. He was moving the way Adam imagined a praying mantis might, an insect he had only seen in books. “I can’t be certain how far from the last station we’ve come. We are looking for the next electrical relay maintenance station. If it hasn’t been damaged by the attackers, we should be able to get up to the surface from there. There will be a small building partly underground with an abundance of emergency equipment. If we’re really lucky, there’ll be a service vehicle and a portable generator to power it up sufficiently to take us fairly quickly to the next stations.”

Adam stayed well clear of the potentially dangerous electrified rail until Ueland signalled that the thick steel power source was disconnected and it was safe to come in contact with it.

“It could possibly reset later, but with the damage behind us, and the destruction of the Manuhome, it’s unlikely. Anyway, if it ever did power up, the lights would come up at the same time and we could hear the power snapping and surging through the line. There would be a powerful humming noise. Lots of warning signs telling us to stay away.”

Then Adam and Ueland turned back to where the others waited and Ueland left him and approached Blanchfleur.

The two began to talk quietly as they separated themselves from the rest of the group. Adam fell back gradually behind them until he was near Alice and Tish. They began moving then, following Blanchfleur and Ueland as they all stumbled carefully along the concrete and dirt floor between the three tracks. They slowly moved farther and farther away from their abandoned railcar and the destroyed city.

Adam worked hard to avoid the two insiders opposite him, which wasn't difficult as they huddled together in the damp darkness, just as anxious to shun him as he was to stay away from them.

The two insiders and the young outsider moved in silence on opposite sides of the tunnel, happy to maintain that distance. The hollow tunnel was far from silent. Every footfall rattled and echoed within the concrete confines.

The boy had muddled feelings toward Alice and Tish. Alice had once been Nora's companion. She was also Mayor Blanchfleur's only daughter. Nora had once lived a privileged life in Blanchfleur's house and at their summer place. Tish was about the same age as he was. She seemed quiet and she was very pretty, as was her mother: same blond hair, same eyes. Tish had a smaller, turned-up nose, which he liked in spite of himself. But he knew nothing about her, except that she'd looked back and across at him several times, worried and curious. Alice seemed young, much younger than his mother, although they, too, must be about the same age.

She seemed nice enough. And Mabon and Nora once told him they owed their lives to Alice because she'd stopped Blanchfleur's Rangers from killing his parents as they fled the valley following Blanchfleur's final battle against the old ones. He knew all this, but he still found it hard to like her. Sometimes she had been mean to Nora, though they'd been good friends. And he wished Tish would stop turning around and looking at him. It made him uncomfortable.

Tish had overheard part of the horrible battle between the Rangers and the old outsiders. She had been outside the open door of her grandmother's control room where the mayor monitored Ranger activities. Tish didn't think it had been fair the way the Rangers were sent to attack the old people. She also knew about the fight between her mother and her grandmother.

All her life she had been told of the evils of the old world before Aahimsa even existed, about how the outsiders had killed and mistreated insiders, making war all over the world, how the insider cities had brought years of peace and security for insiders in cities all over the world.

This boy, this Adam, seemed small and ordinary, just like she was. And yet he had fought in the battle against the powerful Rangers along with some old men and may even have killed and injured enough of them to allow his family to get away. She turned around to look at him again, but this time her mother happened to glance over at her and told her to stop bothering the boy. Then her mother turned around to look at him for herself. Tish twisted around again and Adam looked away, focusing his attention up high on the walls of the tunnel.

The air was getting harder to breathe and more and more rotten as they walked along. Adam wondered if the lack of power meant there wouldn't be enough clean air. He was still worrying about that after walking what seemed another eternity since they had set out. He saw a small metal sign, caked with dirt, about halfway up the tunnel wall on his right. He stepped over close enough to see what it said. It read: "1 KM. NEXT RELAY STN."

"Doctor Ueland," he called. "There's a distance sign here." He watched as everyone stopped and turned to him.

"Can you see what it says, Adam?" Ueland asked.

Adam told him and the doctor said, "Good stuff. One more kilometre to the station, where we should be able get a breath of fresh air and a bit of sunlight, maybe even some decent water to drink. Let's pick up the pace."

"I'm getting tired," said Alice. She was standing close enough to Adam that their eyes met. He could sense her discomfort at their eye contact. Adam held her gaze, growing more confident. He could see why his mother had been drawn to her. He could only think of how he owed her a lot for saving his parents from almost certain death at the hands of the Rangers.

Ueland glanced at Blanchfleur and then turned to Alice. "Yes, we're all tired, but I'd rather not sleep on this filthy rail bed tonight. We can get to shelter and comfort in fifteen minutes even if we go slowly. There should be water and plenty of clean blankets and a warmer place where we can probably be safe and comfortable for at least the next few hours. But if you really would prefer to camp here, we can."

"We'll go on. It makes no sense to stop now," said Blanchfleur. "You'll have to toughen up, Alice. There's a long, hard road ahead, if we're lucky."

Alice looked unhappy. "And if we're not?"

Blanchfleur turned to Ueland, who said nothing. The mayor of the ruined city said, "Then there's no rush, unless you want to stay alive. The only other option means surrender or certain death for all of us here, or perhaps both. In my opinion, we had better get a move on and be glad we have this choice."

Adam was pleased she was so decisive and was surprised at her tone of voice. The insider spoke with some authority, but it was the authority of a kind parent. It reminded him of Nora and Mabon. Her voice sounded just as his parents would have sounded if they were still at home in the Happy Valley. It didn't sound like the voice of an evil murderer. She looked at him with interest. He thought for just a moment that she looked on him with a certain motherly kindness, but he was probably mistaken.

He realized for the first time that while they had until very recently been mortal enemies, they were now together and all of them needed to evade the people who had attacked the Manuhome and Aahimsa. They were now outsiders, all of them. He didn't have any idea why Mayor Blanchfleur was escaping from her own city. He did know she made him nervous. If her look wasn't kindness, was she laughing at him about things she knew that he and Ueland didn't?

And where were Nora and Mabon? Would they know what was happening to the city and to him if they were still alive? Or were they already dead? Was he on his own, surrounded by all of their mortal enemies?

The minutes sped by and soon Ueland had stopped. He shone his flashlight on a rusty metal door in the wall of the tunnel on which the words "DANGER HIGH VOLTAGE" were painted in cracked and bubbled red paint. The doctor fumbled in the pocket of his knee-length wool coat and pulled out a set of keys. He held the small plastic flashlight in his mouth and flicked through the keys until he found the one he wanted. Then he put the key into the brass lock. After wiggling the key back and forth a few times, it turned a quarter turn in the lock and the doctor yanked open the heavy door on its complaining hinges.

He flicked a light switch and nothing happened. "Adam," he said. "Climb up the stairs and try the upper door. It usually isn't locked. If it opens, it's early enough that there should still be some light coming in from outside through the skylight and the small side windows."

Adam walked past the others, who pulled back quickly as if he were infectious, and hurried up the short stairs. Ueland shone his light past him and he found a door handle and pushed down the thumb lever. He pulled on the handle at the same time and was temporarily blinded by the brightness of the light that entered the stairwell from the room outside the door after all this time in the darkened tunnel.

"Go into the room and we'll come on up," Ueland said.

Adam entered the room and, after a few moments of blinking, his eyes finally adjusted to the light. The room was hot and stuffy, although the air smelled much better that what they'd been breathing in the tunnel. The room was large enough to serve as a house for a large family. Along one wall, opposite the door, where there were no windows, sat a large metal console covered in an impressive and confusing array of switches and dials. On either side of the console there were doors — one on the right marked "STORES," and the other, on the left of the console, marked "PRIVATE." There were small piano-style windows in two side walls, and on the fourth wall hung two large charts, one showing the local section of the underground tunnel in detail and the other showing a larger portion of the tunnel system. The maps didn't look new and the room itself looked as if it hadn't been visited in a long while.

"What time is it?" asked Tish. "I'm hungry and thirsty."

Ueland reached inside his topcoat, and then into the inside breast pocket of his suit coat, and pulled out a gold pocket watch on a long golden chain. He flipped open the metal cover. "It's not quite noon," he said.

"I can't believe it's only noon," Alice said. "I'm sleepy and tired." Her round face appeared as pretty as ever in spite of her fatigue. Her eyes looked tired, but they had lost none of their power.

"It's been a difficult day," said Ueland, aware of Alice's loveliness, which never failed to warm his heart. "We all had a rude awakening early this morning. None of us went to bed expecting to be attacked."

Adam found himself beside the console while the adults shuffled about and studied the wall charts. He drifted to the wall where a long couch sat tight against varnished wooden wainscoting. In front of the couch was a stack of fashion magazines on a rectangular wooden coffee table. The table was a dark brown colour and covered with thick, lumpy varnish. A dirty red toolbox sat next to the magazines and beside it, some sort of electrician's testing device. He sat down on the edge of the middle cushion with his hands resting on his knees.

"I'm thirsty, too," Adam said, "and hungry." He looked toward the girl, who glared at him, then looked down at the red-and-white checkerboard of the tile floor.

"We don't have much food," Ueland said. "Just the emergency rations from the railcar. There could be a small quantity of preserved and dried food here in storage. We'll go easy on what we have for now until we can find something more substantial. But I'm soon going to try and fire up the emergency generator and see if the water pump still functions properly. If you see any overhead lights come on in here anywhere at any time, switch them off at once. We don't want to show any lights, day or night; they could be observed from the sky above or anyplace outside. If we can get some water, and maybe a candy bar each, we can get things set up for a decent night's sleep."

"Sleep?" said Blanchfleur as she ran a brush through her hair. She finished quickly and continued, smirking. "Do you think we could ever sleep out here?"

"No. But if things are as I remember, we might not be all that badly off. Leave it to me."

Blanchfleur stuffed her brush in her oversized purse and pointed at the map. "Where to from here?" she asked.

"Let's leave that until the morning. We have a few more hours until it gets dusky. I'd like to get things working here and get set up for the night before it becomes too dark. We can plan things tomorrow."

Ueland went to the console and inserted another of his keys. He pushed a button and they heard a motor somewhere under them turning over very slowly.

"The battery is low," he said. "I'll try again."

This time it growled and turned even more slowly. "One more chance," he said, "and then we're out of luck for the moment."

The starter groaned and whined as its power faded. Adam looked around the room. Everyone seemed to be holding their breath and slowly giving up hope on the generator ever starting, when suddenly it roared to life and the huge console in front of Ueland came on. Indicator lights lit up across the console, as did bulbs overhead as Adam sprang from the couch and turned off the switches on the wall beside the door marked "STORES."

"Good work, Adam," Ueland said over his shoulder. "Glad you were paying attention."

Ueland turned off most of the switches on the panel ahead of him as quickly as he could as the roar of the generator settled and quieted considerably. He walked to the door marked "PRIVATE" and stepped inside.

"Come in here," he said. "Hurry!" Adam entered first, followed by Blanchfleur. "Once we're inside I'll put on the lights. There are no windows," Ueland continued. "Come!"

Blanchfleur turned to her daughter and grandchild. "Come on," she said. "It's perfectly safe."

This room, too, was comfortably large. There were two bunk beds bolted to opposing walls. The beds were made up neatly and covered with heavy, clear plastic. Along the back wall ran a kitchen counter and a set of cupboards next to a closed door on the right. Blanchfleur opened a cupboard door and found stacks of white porcelain dishes and cups. She pulled a drawer and lifted out a handful of clean steel cutlery. Alice went to a tall white enamel refrigerator that now hummed loudly with electricity. She looked shattered when she realized its shelves, drawers, and compartments were completely empty. Tish tried another of the upper cupboards, standing on her tiptoes to reach the handle. Inside was an unappetizing variety of canned goods and boxed cereals and mixes. Adam held up an unopened bag of powdered skim milk.

"Yuck," said Tish.

"At least we won't starve," said Adam with a grin.

Blanchfleur laughed in spite of herself. Tish gave Adam a resentful look and closed the cupboard a bit harder than she had intended. Blanchfleur's glaring look toward Tish made it clear that she was disappointed in her granddaughter's rude reaction.

Ueland made his way to the sink in the middle of the cupboard and turned on the cold tap. The water that came sputtering out was rust-coloured but plentiful, and as it continued to pour it rapidly lost its off-putting colour and became clearer and clearer.

"Anyone ready to try some?" asked Ueland, taking five tall glasses from the cupboard on the opposite side of the sink to where Blanchfleur had discovered the porcelain dishes.

Adam gathered his courage and quietly said, "I'll try it."

The water was cool and tasted quite good, so he happily drank the glass clean and handed it back to Ueland, who refilled it for him.

Alice picked up a glass then and passed it to Ueland. He filled it and Alice handed it over to her mother.

"Thanks," said the mayor and carried it over to Tish. Tish drank it quietly. Ueland filled glasses for Alice and Blanchfleur and then for himself before turning off the tap.

"Now," he said. "Let's think about the sleeping arrangements and decide who goes where. First, though, I want you to know I'll be happy to take the couch outside." He paused for a minute. Then he seemed to have a new idea. "On second thought, I have decided how we'll do it." There was more silence as the others waited to hear his plan. "I'm going to sleep on the couch." He picked up a down duvet and a pillow from a stack of linen and blankets in the lower cupboard at the right end. "You folks can work it out...four people, four bunks. Sounds simple enough. And by the way, the door on the left of the cupboards is a small but adequate washroom. The door on the right is for equipment and parts storage. Once you've decided where to sleep you can come out and talk or go straight to bed. It is pretty early, but it's been a difficult day." He left the room, closing the door behind him.

Adam had no idea what to do or say, so he was glad when Tish spoke first.

"I want to sleep over here with my mother," she said, standing on Alice's right, in front of the bunks along the left wall. She stood with feet apart and arms crossed and Adam understood her clear message that it was decided in her mind. He didn't care. He smiled at her and shrugged as if to say it was fine.

Blanchfleur also shrugged. She turned to Adam. "I guess that leaves us as bunkies. Unless one of us wants to sleep on the floor. Do you want top or bottom? Although I might mention that I'm not much for climbing up those little ladders, or down them for that matter." She walked to the bunk beds attached to the right wall.

"I don't mind the top. But I'm not ready to go up yet. I may visit the doctor until it gets dark," said Adam.

"I may try out the coffee machine here," said Blanchfleur, a little awkwardly. She was very aware how the boy must feel about her. It must feel strange to the child to be bunking with one of his mortal enemies. "I noticed a sealed bag of ground coffee in the cupboard. Take your time. If I'm asleep, don't worry about bothering me when you climb up top. I'll take the plastic covers off both our beds. Goodnight, young fellow."

Adam was growing more and more confused. This day was so weird. Everything had become weird now. He had a terrible headache. He didn't know what to think or what he was supposed to do anymore. "Goodnight," he said, then gave an awkward wave and hurried out the door to visit Doctor Ueland.

Chapter 8: Toward the Abandoned East

Nora and Mabon didn't sleep long. After they descended from atop one of the mountains of debris surrounding the immense crater that had been the Manuhome, they managed to doze enough to restore some of their energy. Nora woke him up, and, already dressed in his dirty clothes from the previous day, he set out with Nora and Lucky at a fairly brisk pace. The night was clear, and overhead a thin sliver of moon gave enough light for them to move safely over the irregular ground and mixed vegetation that grew wild here down close to the lakeside.

They took turns glancing skyward, seeking any sign of aircraft or drones or the quick light path of a passing satellite. The satellite was not overly dangerous unless it passed almost directly overhead. Even if that happened, it took a long time for the controllers to send out a response to whatever had been sighted. Drones or aircraft were a very different matter as the former came armed with deadly weapons and the other with both weapons and kill bots, those nasty, armed, and programmed robots, or police. And where human ground forces were concerned, they had to be quite close by, even if equipped with infrared goggles.

Mabon had explained how the Rangers rarely wore the goggles on patrol for the insiders, as they felt more vulnerable when they wore them. The goggles were useful when approaching a stationary target or when the target was close enough for sniper fire. But when wearing them there was always the uncomfortable feeling that someone was behind you or above you where you could not see them. Better vision made you blind sometimes. He realized after having mentioned the Rangers that the insiders' nasty forest police were no longer a threat — they were either dead or running for their lives.

Nora and Mabon walked until they were nearly exhausted and then began to look for safe shelter. The day was beginning to brighten and they both knew it was time. Off in the far distance they could see a small building with a satellite dish on its roof. It could be a military or police station; best to avoid it.

Lucky seemed interested in the building and wanted to explore. Mabon had to call him several times to get him to follow them off to the right into a small clump of willows where they could rig a tarp and get some sleep through the daylight hours. They set up camp, ate sparingly of their meagre supplies, and, still depressed but exhausted, fell asleep.

They were awakened in the dark several hours later by the intermittent roar of waves of aircraft passing almost directly overhead in the direction of the Manuhome. They held one another tight, their eyes on the blinking red, green, and white navigation lights of the snarling transport aircraft until they finally disappeared to the southwest. The two lovers had feared at first that they might have somehow been the target and prey of these invaders, though there was little logic in this notion. For one thing, there were far too many planes. They had no sooner begun to feel relief when they heard distant sounds of another series of explosions in an area well to the south of where the Manuhome had been.

"What is going on?" asked Mabon. "I don't understand." He continued to stare in the direction of the explosions. The sky overhead was clear and the firmament was awash with brilliant stars. A thin sliver of moon gradually gave him a view of Nora's much beloved face. Those eyes, their specks of gold reflecting the moonlight and the stars, and the lips he could taste just by looking at them. He was startled that she seemed to be smiling. What was there to smile about?

"I wonder," she said. "I wonder what this means. Could it be possible that somehow Ueland managed to get some of his workers out of the Manuhome? If so, and I can't imagine what else these bombers are doing, it means that Ueland and Adam could still be out there somewhere. Oh, Mabon, there is still hope, isn't there?"

Mabon didn't know exactly how to answer. Yes, it could mean they were alive. If so, they were perhaps being killed at this moment. But maybe they were somewhere else, safe…maybe.

"Yes," he said. "There is always hope." He smiled back at her and, leaning toward her, really tasted her soft, warm lips.

They embraced for a long, delicious moment, somehow feeling much better, even with this meagre serving of possibilities. Nora held Mabon as his eyes scanned the southern horizon, which now had taken on a red hue as the explosions continued.

"Oh no!" he said, looking rapidly around.

"What?" said Nora, her voice full of fresh-born alarm.

"Have you seen Lucky?" he asked, stepping in and around the tarp-covered lean-to where they had been sleeping. There was no sign of the dog. Where had he gone?

Chapter 9: A Lucky Night

Ueland was sitting upright on the edge of the couch under the piano windows when Adam came through the door. Light from moon and stars crept in from the sky outside.

The boy let out a sigh, as if relieved to be out of the room with the insiders. Ueland could understand something of what he was feeling. He watched the boy as he crossed the room to where the charts hung on the wall. Ueland realized the charts that far from the windows would be difficult, if not impossible, to see properly.

"Don't switch on any lights," the doctor reminded the boy.

Adam nodded, his finger on the large chart, his eyes close up to it. "Where are we?" he asked.

Ueland smiled and stood, stretching and shaking off his stiffness and fatigue. They were all of them operating under unimaginable stress, their worlds suddenly ripped apart at the seams. And now all that was gone, too. It was no wonder he wanted to know where they were.

The chart before which Adam stood showed the eastern third of what was called Isabella's Land, and Adam had his finger planted on Aahimsa, the most northerly city of Northern Isabella Land.

"You are pointing almost at where we are. We're not far from what was Aahimsa. Come look at this other chart; it covers a much smaller area in greater detail," said Ueland as they stepped to the second chart. "Here's the line of the tunnel. Here's the service building where we are right now. We're very close to the city where you were born, as you can see."

Adam looked over the detailed area of the map that represented the City of Aahimsa. He had never seen a map of the city where Nora had lived at the time of his birth. The city where he had been born of his mother Minn outside of the determination. Where he was destined to be terminated, and from which Nora had fled, carrying him in her young arms.

He was amazed at how big the city was, with its vast maze of streets and its many parks. It looked so beautiful and luxurious. He wondered what it looked like now, after the explosions they had heard as they had fled.

"Where are we going?" Adam asked now.

Ueland wasn't sure what to tell him. "We don't have many options at the moment," he said. "We're north of Aahimsa and the lake is to the east of us. The best climate is to the south, but that is where the largest cities of the World Federation of Cities lie. Much of the territory outside the cities isn't safe or fit to live in and it is closely watched by the Federation. I'm thinking we will follow this rail tunnel to the north and then swing east. There is good land there, but it is a very wild and cold place, especially in winter. I'm not in charge here; the others will have a major say in our final decision," he said. "So this is just speculation."

"You mean Blanchfleur," said Adam.

"I mean the others...all of them," said Ueland. He sounded tired and somewhat annoyed.

"Why do we have to help them?" asked Adam, his voice angry and bitter. "They tried to kill us."

"Not now," said Ueland, holding up his hand to stop the conversation. "It's too long a story and it won't help anyone to bring all that up now. Perhaps there'll be time for such discussions later."

"Perhaps," said Adam, his face showing his contempt for their fellow travellers.

"Perhaps. I'm sorry, Adam, but I have to get some rest. Go and get some sleep. We'll need to be fresh."

"Can't I stay here with you?"

"There's no room."

"I want to stay out here," insisted the boy.

"Okay," said Ueland. "I give up. I'll sleep in the room, you take the couch. Don't touch anything. See you in a few hours."

Adam nodded. He didn't want to stay here alone in this big room, but he certainly didn't want to be in there with them. He watched as Ueland entered the room where the others slept, and then he dragged his weary feet to the couch and burrowed beneath the thick covers.

Adam awoke later to the sound of large aircraft flying overhead. He stood on the couch and shuffled across to the window on the left. The sky was clear and full of stars, there was moonlight, and he could see jet trails streaking across the sky. He wondered what was going on.

He looked out across the grounds that surrounded this small building where they had all been sleeping. Outside, he thought he saw something move, off to his right — some kind of animal creeping toward the building. His heart leapt. It was a dog, a big old dog. Was it possible? The dog came closer and disappeared from view below him, and then reappeared off to his left. The dog looked up toward the window. The boy could see that the dog was barking. But he couldn't hear.

He felt his heart pounding as if it might burst, and his cheeks were getting damp. It was Lucky. It was his dog. And if Lucky was out there, perhaps Nora and Mabon were close by. He had to figure out how to get outside. He had to wake Ueland.

Chapter 10: Lucky Calls Them

Nora and Mabon rose, still half asleep in the darkness, and meticulously searched the area around their little camp. They found no sign of their missing dog. They could still hear the deadly rumblings of warfare to the southwest and knew that the planes were far enough away that they were safe from attack for a little while. As long as there were explosions in the distance they felt they could have a look around. The attackers to the south of the Manuhome would have dropped seeker drones below them to search for human targets. And when the planes left they might leave the drones behind to continue their search. Of course, there were no guarantees.

"We should get under cover again as soon as possible. The attackers will be returning to their bases soon and we could be seeing some drones up this way sometime after that," said Mabon.

"Okay," said Nora. But her eyes continued to search all around them.

"Listen," said Mabon. "Shush!"

They stood in silence for more than a minute before Nora heard it faintly in the distance to the west: the unmistakeable sound of their dog barking at something. Not a threatening bark but a bark of recognition, an excited barking.

"Come on," she said, running in the direction of the sound.

Mabon gazed skyward as he followed her, making sure that there was nothing obvious watching their movements from overhead, knowing that if they were spotted, the forces of the World Federation would soon be on them with the full force of its killing anger.

Chapter 11: Dangerous Encounter

Adam threw open the door marked "PRIVATE" and dashed inside into the deep darkness. He didn't want to wake everyone by turning on the overhead light, but once inside he had to navigate with the meagre illumination seeping past the door behind him from whatever lighting the starry sky projected through the small windows of the control room. It just wasn't enough. As a result he correctly guessed the approximate location of the bunk bed on the right that he had recently deserted and where Ueland would likely be sleeping above Mayor Blanchfleur, but in his haste and anxiety, he tripped on the lower bunk and fell across the sleeping form of Alice's mother.

Blanchfleur had just fallen into a restless sleep and was dreaming about the horrors that had so recently overtaken her city and her homelands. Adam's landing on her had been incorporated into her nightmare as an attacking, vengeful Ranger and the mayor reacted violently, throwing the boy onto the floor and screaming a chill-inducing warning to all around her.

Adam gathered himself gradually from the floor and made his way to the dimly lit doorway, heart bursting with an odd blend of terror and his rekindled excitement after the sighting of his dog, Lucky, who could still be somewhere just outside the window, waiting to be rescued. As he reached the doorway, he flicked on the brilliant overhead light.

Ueland had dropped to the floor and Blanchfleur had returned to the present from her dream-befuddled mind. She pushed aside her covers and stood up beside the bed. Alice and Tish sat up on their bunks, their covers pulled up close to their chins.

"Lucky is outside," Adam said, his impatient voice filled with new hope and excitement. "We have to go get him now."

"Lucky," said Alice, just waking up. "Who is Lucky?"

"Adam, I'm sorry. I was dreaming. I hope you are all right?" said Blanchfleur.

"I'm fine," he said. "I'm great! It's okay." He said to her and ran to Ueland. "We have to get outside. Mabon and

Nora could be alive. They could be outside, too."

"Who are all these people he's talking about?" asked Tish.

"His parents," said Ueland, "and their dog."

"How do you know they're really there?" asked Alice. "Maybe you were dreaming?"

"No, I was wide awake. The planes woke me up when they passed overhead."

"What planes?" asked Blanchfleur, her face alert and suddenly concerned.

"Big, loud planes," said Adam. "Going that way." He pointed to the southwest. "Come on, Doctor Ueland. Let's go out before Lucky leaves. Please."

"What about the planes?" Alice asked. "Aren't you worried about the planes seeing you?"

"We'll go now before the planes come back," said Ueland. "Come on!" He headed out the door, Adam close behind. Blanchfleur followed on his heels.

"Which way were those planes headed?" Ueland asked.

Adam looked toward the window above the couch, and then he pointed.

"Oh dear," muttered Ueland.

"What is it?" asked Blanchfleur. Adam turned to look at her. Her eyes were fixed on Ueland, who stopped for a moment.

"Some of my workers got out through escape tunnels I had dug in case of such an emergency," he said to the mayor. "The eyes must have found some of them."

"You think of everything, don't you?" Blanchfleur said, appearing somewhat amused.

"Not exactly," he said. "I wish it were so." He turned back

to Adam. "We'll have to watch for aircraft and anything that moves. Come on!" He strode quickly to the door marked "STORES," took out his keys, and unlocked it. He turned to Blanchfleur. "Get the others to keep the inside door closed or turn out the light. Anyone could be out here, and if they see any sign of light coming from this station, we could have very serious problems."

Blanchfleur ran back to where the bedroom door stood ajar and flicked off the light. "Leave this off until we get back or make sure the door stays shut when the light is on," she said, and slammed the door. She followed Ueland and Adam into the storeroom. They closed the door. They were in a small corridor. Ueland pulled a small flashlight from his pocket and shone it on the lock of a heavy, windowless door. "Stay back," he said. He unlocked the door and turned off the flashlight. The door opened easily, the hinges creaking softly. Dim, creamy moonlight seeped inside. The boy and the two adults stepped outside, staying close against the side of the grey metal building. They heard the sound of an animal, breathing heavily, rushing toward them.

Blanchfleur pulled a small weapon from her pocket and aimed it out into the surrounding darkness. She moved the pistol from side to side.

"No," said Ueland. "Put that thing away." He stood directly in front of her. Adam briefly wondered why he wasn't afraid of her or her gun.

Then Adam turned and ran away from the building into the darkness of the night, and suddenly it was dog and boy welded in an ecstasy of chaotic noise and activity. "Lucky, Lucky, Lucky," the boy said over and over like a song of joy, and then they were silent and still, and then he cried.

And suddenly there were other, heavier sounds of running as footsteps approached. Blanchfleur's weapon reappeared. The others shrank close against the wall. Then Nora appeared and Ueland jerked Blanchfleur's weapon from her hand and roughly yanked her back beside him. Next Mabon appeared, followed by Adam and the dog, the whole family united once again, dissolved into a sea of tender tears, and muffled sounds of unbridled joy.

Ueland interrupted them, pointing to the southwest, where sounds of approaching aircraft were growing louder by the moment. "Let's get ourselves inside. With luck we will have lots of time to reacquaint ourselves and tell our many stories. And we can try to turn all this into something positive for all of us — not an easy thing to imagine, but who knows."

The doctor held the door for Mabon, Adam, Nora, and then the dog, who hesitated a moment before Adam said, "Come, Lucky. It's safe in here." The dog entered, tail wagging wildly, and ran to the deliriously happy boy. Then Blanchfleur entered. They stood in the doorway a moment, aware of the ominous roar of the World Council's approaching attack planes.

"Find a place to sit for a while. Stay close to a wall and don't move. We don't want those planes or their drones picking up any movement or reflected light in here. I'm going to kill the generator for a bit. If anyone wants to talk, keep it really quiet." He walked to the console and flicked a switch. The room dropped to a much more profound silence and seemed darker somehow, dark enough that the windows over the couch seemed to glow with almost magical light.

Nora and Mabon sat on either side of Adam, squeezing him and ruffling his scraggly brown hair. They restrained their excitement enough that Lucky's tail brushing against everything and everyone was the loudest sound in the room.

From where Blanchfleur and Ueland sat they watched the flashing lights as a string of passing aircraft returned across the lake to some distant base. They waited a while after the last few passed before Ueland stood and restarted the generator, whose starter battery, now fully charged, turned the big engine over rapidly. It started quickly and loudly and instantly settled into a comforting roar.

"We'll leave the lights for now," he said. "Alice and Tish are trying to sleep in the adjoining room. Blanchfleur can join them if she wishes. Adam can return to the couch. There's an empty bunk for someone in there. I'll get blankets from the storeroom for anyone who wants them."

"I'm happy with a blanket," said Blanchfleur. "Let the others get some sleep. I can't sleep anyway, thinking of all those lost workers and my poor citizens."

"I'm staying out here with Adam," said Nora, her voice almost purring with happiness. "I never want to leave him again."

"Me, too," said Mabon. "Your citizens are probably safe enough. More than I can say about the old ones and those workers."

"Suit yourselves; I'll get a pile of blankets. But the floor isn't too warm," Ueland said. "I'm going back to bed in the other room. The lower bunk will be empty."

"I'm sorry about the old ones and about everything else. And the workers." She paused. "What do you mean about my citizens being safe?"

"Nora and I watched many dozens of massive transport copters loaded with evacuated insiders fly out of the city for hours, crossing and re-crossing the lake, before planes blew up Aahimsa," Mabon said.

Adam spoke directly to the mayor. "If you really are sorry about what happened to the old ones and nearly happened to us, why did you do it?"

"I'll never make you understand. The answers never really make sense. I was trying to save the city. I was trying to save the Manuhome and all the workers. I was even trying to save Ueland. But I failed," said Blanchfleur.

"Are you trying to blame all this on us?" asked Nora,

"No, not blame," said Blanchfleur. "When you left Aahimsa and Alice, when you took baby Adam outside the city, you may have sparked all of this violence. But the Federation of City Councils and the World Council were looking for an excuse to destroy all of us, the city and the Manuhome. Because of their recent improvements in the cloning process they no longer needed our reproductive fluids and they wanted to destroy our cheap labour. We were keeping outsiders alive and we were seen as a constant threat to the Federation and its policies. Besides, how can I blame you for wanting to survive? I expect you hate me and I understand. I think my own daughter hates me. In many ways I hate myself. I tried to do what I thought was for the best. I did it for love. So you were the spark, Nora;

you and Adam. But you are not to blame. The blame must be shared by all of us for failing to find a real solution to our violence."

"I want to ask a favour," said Nora, her voice pleading to be understood.

"Yes, what is it? If I can do you a favour, I will gladly do it," said Blanchfleur.

"Okay. Can you leave us alone as a family for a little while?" asked Nora.

Blanchfleur got up from the floor and folded her blanket. She walked toward the door marked "PRIVATE" and opened it. She paused and turned to them. "Goodnight," she said. "I'll see you folks in a few hours."

Chapter 12: Decision Time

Mabon rose from the couch. "I want to get our things," he said.

"Wait," said Nora. "We have a decision to make before the others return. Do we stay with the others or get away from them now?"

"Adam, would you be happy if our whole family left right now, and headed out by ourselves?" asked Mabon.

Adam shrugged. He thought it was a great idea, now that they were back together as a family. Strangely, though, he felt funny about leaving Ueland and the insiders. Doctor Ueland knew a lot of things that might help them get away and help them start up new lives somewhere. And now that Mabon and Nora were here with Lucky, he was feeling like they all could get along together.

“I thought Alice was your friend. Aren’t you even going to say hello to her?” he asked, looking at his mother. “And didn’t you say she saved your life?”

“But her mother was the one who tried to kill all of us in the first place,” said Nora. She glanced at Mabon. He hadn’t said a word. “What do you think?”

“Ueland helped us,” he said, “and Alice helped, too. I don’t think they’ll force us to stay if we decide to leave. But I think we owe them a chance to talk over the future with us. Together we might be stronger. Either way, we’ll have to figure out how to survive until we can find someplace safe to settle. I think we should stay. But it might be better to leave our weapons and supplies hidden for now. Let’s wait till morning to think about it. Perhaps we will travel separately but stay connected somehow. Let’s talk tomorrow and see what everyone has to say.”

“I agree with Mabon, Mom,” said Adam, his face adult and determined.

“So you don’t mind me seeing Alice?” Nora asked Mabon, taking the big man’s hand in hers.

“No. I want you to see her,” said Mabon. “You owe her at least that. It must have been hard for her when you left without explanation all those years ago.”

“What about Blanchfleur?” asked Nora, her eyes intent on his face.

“What about her?” he said. He turned his eyes to her. She always found it difficult to look directly into those depths without becoming hypnotized by them. But she was determined to ask her question.

"She tried to kill us all. How can we treat her like an equal travelling companion?"

"She was the mayor," he said. "She was just doing her job, trying to save the city and her people."

"And all the workers and Ueland," said Adam. "It's weird. It's like she and Ueland are friends. The doctor and I saved her and her family from getting captured or killed. Ueland and Blanchfleur must have planned it, because he knew where they'd be waiting. And Ueland was fooling her all the time. He protected the old ones. I've been trying to figure it out and it doesn't make sense. None of it makes any sense."

"Okay," said Nora after a long pause and a breathy sigh. "We stay long enough to talk to the others about plans. Then we decide. Let's try to get some sleep so we can at least think straight."

"Okay," said Adam. "I can do that."

Mabon nodded and put an arm around each of them. "I'm happy," he said. "I'm so very happy that we're all together again. For now that's enough. I don't have to understand everything. Sometimes understanding doesn't help much."

Nora felt better for hearing Mabon's words. She felt happy, too, as she and Adam settled down on the couch and Mabon, nearby, wrapped himself in several soft blankets, a cushion from the couch under his head. He was soon asleep, his regular, mild snoring somehow comforting to both Adam and Nora. Adam slept next, happier than he'd been since they fled the valley.

Nora lay awake for a short while, thoughts of Alice and her mother sweeping in and out of her mind. She had briefly met Tish when the child was younger. She wondered if the girl would remember that day when she found Nora bleeding and helpless near the concrete obelisk. She wondered whether Alice would still be as beautiful as she used to be; a dozen years can bring many changes to any woman's appearance, especially a mother's. She, herself, had changed a great deal, and she hadn't even given birth to Adam.

Moments later Nora fell to dreaming of the peaceful days they'd all spent together in the valley.

Chapter 13: Hard Decisions

Ueland stood in the dark stairway leading up from the tunnel, removed his keys from his pocket, put the small red flashlight between his teeth, and, by moving his head slowly, aimed it at the tarnished lock. He inserted the key and turned it slowly until with a satisfying click it opened. He then removed the key, wiped it against his trouser leg, and placed the ring of keys in the left front pocket of those suit pants. He opened the door slowly, trying to keep the squeaks from the rarely used hinges to a minimum. But his efforts were in vain as the rusty door squealed in protest. He stepped gingerly inside and he saw that Adam was wide awake and gazing at him from his place on the couch. Mabon and Nora were also awake again and alert, and watching him. They all, however, looked surprised and startled.

"I thought you were sleeping inside with the others," said Adam.

"I had been. But I only managed to sleep a very short while. I had machinery to set up down below. I've finished with all that and we can leave whenever we're ready," said the doctor.

"But we're going to have time to talk things over first?" said Nora.

"And eat something, maybe," added Adam.

"Yes," said Ueland. "Who wants to go in and wake the others?"

There were no takers. He looked from one to the other and laughed, then crossed the room to the door marked "PRIVATE" and disappeared inside the main sleeping quarters.

"I hope he isn't much longer," said Adam after Ueland had been gone a few long minutes. And almost as if Adam's words were a cue, the door to the inside room opened and Ueland stuck his head into the front room where the family waited.

"I've water boiling for porridge and hot drinks. There's tinned juice and some stale cereals. There's a bit of mouldy cheese and hard tack. It's not much but it will have to do. Wait a minute and everyone will be up, dressed, and ready to talk and then to travel. We'd best not get too comfortable here." He glanced at Nora and then Mabon and Adam. "Not that I expect that there are many of us here who are all that comfortable. But trust me, that's something that will likely improve. A minute or two and then come in."

Chapter 14: New Beginnings (along the lake)

It was decided after some discussion that Mabon and Adam would head out first, as darkness approached, to scout out the camp. Nora would remain to guide the others after an hour or so had passed. Lucky would stay behind with them. Adam would return while Mabon uncovered gear and supplies. Nora would help the others decide what bedding and supplies they could safely and practically bring along. What they left behind would have to be well hidden in the tunnel or outside so it wouldn't lead to their presence being discovered later.

"Okay," said Mabon. He kissed Nora and held her for a moment.

"Be careful," she said. "Both of you." She tried to embrace Adam, who shied away uncomfortably, embarrassed, but smiled nonetheless.

"We will," they said with one voice. Quietly, and with no further fuss, they slipped out the door. Lucky had followed them to the door, but Adam told him to stay with Nora. The old dog settled beside the sofa and after a few moments went back to sleep.

Alice had looked on as Nora said goodbye to Adam and Mabon. She found Nora and Mabon's relationship fascinating, though awkward. It startled her at first, but their tenderness toward one another was obvious and natural, born out of comfort and trust, and heightened by Nora's concern for the possible dangers Adam and Mabon might be facing outside. The cleaner and the boy were impressive, too, neither of them appearing aggressive or threatening to the insiders even for a moment. She had seen the curiosity in the boy's face as he observed her and her daughter, and Tish, though obviously nervous around the outsiders, seemed to share his fascination. And now Alice felt her heart begin to race as Nora approached the building: her Nora, the Nora of her memories, her dreams, and her nightmares.

"Let's get our final packing done," said her former companion, smiling and turning away as she passed by.

Alice stopped, holding Tish back and turning toward Nora. "No, wait," she said. "There are things I want to say to you."

Nora didn't move. "There's no time now." Her face was full of sadness. "Later."

"I'm sorry for how badly I used to treat you, and about the boy." Alice blurted these words and her eyes grew damp. She choked and smothered a sob.

Nora didn't move, but her face softened. "I'm sorry I left you to handle the whole thing. It must have been difficult... but we have to get ready."

"Yes. Let's," agreed Alice. "Come, Tish."

There was an awkward few moments as all gathered around the large mound of sleeping bags and pinned bedrolls and whatever gear they had gathered from the kitchen and the stores. They were soon all business.

"Can we manage all this?" asked Alice looking over the huge pile.

Nora laughed, then stopped, embarrassed.

"Why are you laughing?" asked Tish.

"I'm nervous," Nora said. "This will be difficult and so disappointing. Perhaps I can ask a question to answer yours: How much can each of you manage? And remember that we have to carry and set up our own gear. We will be walking and perhaps even running for our lives. We have to stay out of sight and leave as few signs as possible of our having stopped here."

"Let's try not to be nervous around one another if we can," said Alice. "How long do we have before we leave here?"

"Much less than an hour," Nora said.

"What do you suggest? What are you going to take with you?" Alice looked to Nora for guidance.

Nora smiled, realizing that this was all new territory for the insiders. She reached into her jacket pocket and pulled out a pair of scissors and several books of matches, along with a small can opener. She picked up a cloth bag of dried food that included a few small cans.

"What else?" asked Tish.

"Nothing else from this place. I have some underclothes and a sweater and a few personal things in a backpack, and a bow and some arrows with our other things under the trees along by the water."

"So help us. This is hard for us. What should we take?" asked Alice.

"A small backpack or bag. A few clothes. Small things you need. Medicine if you have it. Mabon has a medicine bag. We have a large tarp for shelter and a small axe. You'll want a blanket or bedroll. Something small for a pillow if you need it. A cup, a small plate and utensils, a small knife, a toothbrush. A piece of cloth to wash yourself when you can, some other small cloths, a small towel. Remember that you'll have to help carry your things and your share of our camp gear, etc. We all have to do our share."

"Suitcases?" asked Tish.

"Do you want to carry a suitcase for hundreds of miles over rough terrain?" asked Nora, trying to make them understand without insulting them.

Tish began to cry. Alice felt like joining her; she, too, was taken aback as her expectations were shattered one after another and the reality of their situation was beginning to set in. Up to now they had been on a brief outing away from the security of the city, from their luxurious lives. They had left Aahimsa in the plush comfort of Blanchfleur's private railcar. Even after the explosions that forced them out of the car, they had only travelled briefly in the dank, stuffy tunnel and exited into a relatively comfortable working person's shelter with beds, a kitchen, and even a bathroom with a shower and a toilet. Now they were exiting into the wild, where they would be hunted by the forces of the Federation and Goddess knew what wild creatures.

Alice took little Tish into her embrace and kissed the tears from her cheeks. "Let's get started. That boy will be returning before we know it."

Half an hour later Adam arrived back and helped them pack and organize their few things.

"This is a lot of stuff," he said, and Tish gave him a surly glance. He ignored her and went over the instructions that Mabon had given him before he left the camp. "One of you follow close enough behind me that you can still see me. We'll go in a line, slowly. Mom will go last. No talking and no lights, not even a match. When we get to the camp we'll split up everything we need to carry and begin to walk. The night is mostly cloudy but there is enough light from the sky that we'll have to stay close under the trees."

"How far?" asked Tish, her voice still shaky but somewhat calmer than before.

"Mabon wants to get to the next service building. He doesn't want to be too far behind Blanchfleur and Doctor Ueland. He says at least two hours, maybe three or four. If we don't get there, or if it doesn't look safe, we'll set up camp nearby and try and get some sleep. The bugs don't seem too bad tonight."

"I wondered where they were. How are they getting there? Are they behind us?" said Tish.

"They took some kind of little cars down the tracks in the tunnels. I think they're ahead of us," said Adam.

"Why didn't we all go that way?" asked Tish.

"Ueland thought it better to split up. He was afraid we'd all get trapped if they bombed the tunnels."

Tish didn't like to think about her grandmother and Ueland being in danger. She changed the subject. "What about the bugs?"

"Mabon has a salve that helps," answered Adam, feeling sorry for the girl. "We'll get some when we get to camp."

"What sort of bugs? We had no bugs in Aahimsa," Alice said.

"There are millions of flying bugs like mosquitoes and blackflies and other flies and bees and wasps. Some bite and some sting. Others are annoying, noisy, and pesky when they land on you and crawl on your skin and get in your eyes," said Adam, having no true notion as to how much his words bothered the insiders, since insects had been an everyday part of his world.

Nora sympathized with the insiders. She recalled her first evening in the wild after coming outside the walls with little Adam, before she met Mabon, and just before the attack of the wild dogs that had brought him to her rescue. The biting flies got into her eyes and hair. They bit her mercilessly. They bit the baby Adam, too, though he would have no memory of that at a few months of age. Before the dogs came she had buried herself and the baby under thick wool blankets to keep the bugs at bay. It had helped, but not all that much. Later, after he had rescued them, Mabon had shared his bug repellent and the bugs became almost bearable.

After a time you get used to anything, she thought. But the memories of those first bug attacks were still fresh enough that she pitied the insiders as they were introduced to the worst realities of the wild. They were lucky, though, out here by the lakeshore, where the flies were less of a burden than they were farther inland among the trees and swampland and the wild grasses. "Leave the flies," said Nora. "We'll deal with them when we have to. If we're lucky we won't have flies tonight. If we do we'll get you some fly dope right away."

"Let's move," said Adam. "Stay close. If we get separated, stay in one place and don't call out. We'll be back to get you. Lucky never lets us get lost."

Adam set a moderate pace and the others, Tish, then Alice, and finally Nora and Lucky, stayed close behind. Already Alice and Tish were having trouble with their packs and rolls and gear. They kept shifting things about, grunting or sighing frequently but managing not to say anything that might be heard. Nora would, from time to time, remind them of the severe consequences of making the smallest unnecessary noise.

A short time later they arrived at a thick stand of evergreens and Adam slowed to help them get through the trees between dense, fragrant branches, into deeper darkness where the sky above the trees was barely visible, and after a short trek they stopped inside a small clearing. "We're here," said Adam.

Alice and Tish looked around them and saw nothing but trees. "Where's your camp?" asked Tish.

At that moment Mabon stepped out of the shadows. "Welcome," he said in a soft voice, almost a whisper. "I wish we could have left our camp set up as it was for you to see it. But we're packed and ready to leave. Come and pick up what you can."

"I can't carry all this any farther," said Tish, her small voice in a panic.

"You may have taken too much," said Alice, worried.

"I already left my really good stuff back there," she said, ready to cry.

"I can take some of it," offered Adam. "I have room."

Tish's eyes became pinched and her jaw determined. "I can carry my own stuff," she said. "And I'll help with the other stuff, somehow."

Adam smiled to himself. She was strong in her own way. She would get along fine.

Mabon began to prepare by lifting a large backpack onto his powerful arms, followed by his quivers of arrows, his longbow, and several large bags of food and supplies. Nora did the same with smaller and lighter gear, and the others did their best to follow suit.

Nora stood next to Mabon. "Mabon will lead the way for the first while. Please try to make no unnecessary sounds. Even a grunt or a sigh can let searchers find us, animal, human, or animatronic."

"Has anyone had a problem with insects?" asked Mabon. "If so, let me know. No talk, but you can tug on the clothing of the person in front of you and pass your message quietly along. When I feel a tug I'll stop and we can speak softly. If you hear or see danger, just stop where you are. Adam and Nora and I will teach you safe sounds. For now we can all make a sound like an owl. *Hoo, hoo, hoo,*" said Mabon. "Three times like that and you freeze where you are and do not move. There are lots of us here and if one gets found by the searchers, we are all found. You all know the risks. We will begin now. We will go for what may seem a long way, but this will, unfortunately, be one of our shorter walks."

Tish spoke softly. "If it was light out, could we see any of the city wall from here? If we weren't in these trees..."

Nora spoke. "We're so sorry, Tish. Mabon and I were much closer to the city than this when it exploded. It's completely gone — the city, the Manuhome, everything. There is not even a sign of the walls or any part of the city left. It was dissolved by the big Federation bombs."

Alice and Tish stood speechless. They knew it had been ruined, but this was so much worse than they had imagined.

"We'd better get moving," said a sympathetic Nora, who had known such loss more than once in the past. "Sorry."

Mabon nodded at her and led the overburdened line of walkers away in the direction of their next destination, the next service building. As he strode powerfully along, he wondered how far Ueland and Blanchfleur had gotten as they rode their little electric machine through the dank darkness along the tracks underground. He hoped all was going well and they would all be seeing one another soon.

Chapter 15: Service Building 2

A little more than twenty-five minutes after climbing aboard the service vehicle, following an uneventful but careful ride through the musty, dark tunnel, travelling about ten kilometres, Ueland and Blanchfleur arrived at the underground entrance to the second service tunnel building.

Together, they manoeuvred the small flatbed into its service bay and Ueland connected its charging cables. This underground room was larger and better equipped than the first: there was an abundance of tools and equipment, including a second service vehicle.

"Let's hope there is enough reserve power in the batteries to start up this generator," Ueland said.

"And if not?" Blanchfleur asked.

"I may be able to start the generator with a boost from the service vehicle battery. It is fully charged from the trip up here. Let's go up. And I see there is a small portable gas-powered generator and charger for service call emergencies."

Ueland opened the lower door and they climbed up the short flight of stairs to the upper door, then entered a room that was an exact copy of the previous service building control room, except that the couch was larger and upholstered in blue fabric. The doctor walked to the console and inserted his master key, powered-on the console, then pushed the starter button for the generator. This time the big power source sprung quickly to life.

"What now?" asked Blanchfleur. She stretched and yawned, walked to the large wall chart, and looked it over without speaking.

"We leave it to fully charge the batteries, and then we wait," he said. "Will you be all right if I go below to the workshop a few minutes? There's something I should do." He went out the door. Blanchfleur stepped slowly to one of the high windows above the sofa that looked down over the lake. It was still bright outside and the others may not even have left yet. She decided to grab this opportunity to lie down on the couch and snatch a much-needed rest. Ueland would be puttering around down below; that was his way.

She was glad. She knew no one on the planet more useful to have around at times like these. She was oddly happy to be out of her beloved city. It was gone and her heart was broken in many ways, but she was suddenly free of all its onerous burdens. Free of all she was required to do in order to defend it.

Alice was close by with Tish, and soon she and all her loved ones would be travelling here through the wild, along with Alice's former partner, Nora. The same Nora who had probably been the spark that initiated of all this destruction and death. Adam, the wild boy, whose life Nora rescued from the determination, the illegal son of Minn who had thrown herself from the wall, was also going to be travelling with them.

Mabon, their guide, was obviously a good man. He had been willing to die to help the insider, Minn, even to the extent of breaking the law of contact and condemning himself to almost certain death. He had saved Nora and Adam from many dangers in the wild, and done so much more. She admired them all. They had been her enemies and they had fought a battle to the death. No one had won that battle. No one ever wins such battles. And they hated her. She understood. She was so tired and she noticed for the first time how much her head was aching.

When Ueland came back up from the tunnel, he didn't wake her. He stepped inside the back room, set down his bag of supplies, and put some water in a pot on the stove. After he made and drank his coffee, he inspected the room to see what resources it might provide them, plugged in the other appliances, then lay down and slept a few hours. When he woke he checked his watch and knew it was well after dark. The others would arrive there before long. He had better check and make sure everything was ready for them.

Part 3

Chapter 16: The Enemies Return

Adam, Nora, Mabon, and their fellow travellers in the wild had been forced to stop about half a kilometre from the service building. Nora had heard the snarling overhead engines first, off in the distance, faintly. The flying machines were crossing the lake behind them and once they all were able to see the navigation lights — the red on the left, the green on the right, and the white above — Mabon knew from the noise and the speed that these were helicopters, large troop carriers. And they were heading toward the large, forested area to the south of Aahimsa.

"They're putting some kind of troops, feet on the ground. Going in for the kill," said Mabon. "Everyone lie down and keep perfectly still. But feel free to talk quietly for a few minutes. The racket those metal birds are making will cover up for us."

"What's going on?" Tish asked Alice. "What does he mean, going in for the kill? Killing who?"

"I don't know, Tish," her mother said. But she suspected. This made what was happening even worse and harder to understand.

Adam heard them, too. He said nothing. He knew about the escaping workers, and the start of the bombing of the Manuhome. This was more of the same.

Nora had seen similar helicopters in action before from a safe distance. "They lifted most of the insiders from the city and took them away by helicopter across the lake. Other planes or drones bombed the Manuhome and then destroyed the entire city. These helicopters are doing something else. They aren't bringing insiders back. Aahimsa's gone."

"Why are they killing them?" asked Tish. "What did they do?"

Nora could only shrug. There was no reasonable answer to Alice's daughter's question. "Now they're killing all the escaped Manuhome workers they can find. They want to kill Adam and Mabon and probably me. Maybe all of us, even Blanchfleur." She let that sink in.

"I have a question for Adam and for you, Alice," Nora continued, feeling angry and dumbfounded by Alice's lack of awareness. "Why is Ueland helping Blanchfleur? His actions come as a surprise to me, considering what Adam and Mabon and I have been through with him. And there's another mystery: Why has Blanchfleur protected Ueland in the Manuhome all these years, even after she found out he was regularly lying to her and deceiving her?"

"I don't know," said Alice. "I've wondered about them, too, ever since I was a little girl. How much has Ueland helped you?"

"Lots," said Mabon. "He kept all of us alive. Even while Blanchfleur was trying to kill us."

"She wasn't trying to kill anyone she didn't have to. I hate all the killing. But to be fair to her, she was doing what she had to in order to keep as many outsiders alive as possible."

"That's crazy," said Nora.

"Is it?" asked Alice. "She was sure the Federation was looking for excuses to change Aahimsa into a city like all the others. They wanted an end to ALL outsiders, an end to the Manuhome."

"Do you know that for sure?" asked Nora, incredulous.

"Yes. Think about it," she said. "You decided to leave with Adam. They found Minn's body. The cleaner fled. After that the pressure on my mother to catch you was enormous."

"His name is Mabon," said Adam. "He's not a cleaner now."

Mabon said nothing, just listened, pleased and proud that Adam demanded respect for him from Alice.

Alice continued. "Sorry. Mabon disappeared. The Central Council was furious. Mom tried everything she could to settle them down. Things were getting quiet when they found the valley with the old ones and the boy and you, Nora."

"So are you blaming me, Adam, and Mabon for all this?" asked Nora her voiced pinched and angry.

"I don't blame anyone. This is the way it has always been with us, I'm beginning to think," Alice said.

"What do you mean?" asked Nora. "Who do you mean by 'us'?" Her voice was more even, conversational.

"I mean us — people. We try to find peace and agreement but we always find a way to disagree, to hurt one another, to fight, to kill. We fought against the tyranny of the outsider and won and now we begin to fight one another. And what good will it do to run away?"

"We'll be alive," said Adam, a smile on his young face.

"For how long?" asked Alice, her voice dark with fear.

"We'll have to wait and see," interrupted Mabon. "Let's get going before those noisy metal birds come back. The others will be waiting for us and wondering. Come on. We're all alive now, and every day is a new beginning." He gave Nora his hand and they gathered their gear and started on their way. The others followed as quickly as they could.

Twenty minutes later Mabon turned the key in the outer door of the service building. The interior was dark as an underground tunnel and it was beginning to rain outside. All five of the travellers and Lucky followed the short corridor that led to the front room and stepped inside.

"There's nobody here," said Tish once they were all inside.

"We're here," said a mature feminine voice from their left, down low. Lucky barked at the unexpected voice deep in the dark of the room.

"Hush, Lucky," said Adam. "It's only Mayor Blanchfleur."

Tish had recognized her grandmother's sleepy voice. She moved immediately toward the sound and settled next to Blanchfleur, smiling up at her as her eyes adjusted to the meagre light that entered through the narrow windows overhead.

"Can we put on some lights?" Tish asked.

"Not unless we go inside the bedroom," said Mabon. "I can hear the generator running, so we can go inside there, close the door, and turn on some lights. We can't be too careful. We saw and heard helicopters heading toward the Manuhome. They'll be coming back this way after a bit. We can't allow any light to show on the outside or they'll attack us. I wonder if we shouldn't shut down the generator for the moment."

"Where's Doctor Ueland?" asked Adam, looking around as his eyes became accustomed to the sparse light.

"I don't know. I had a lie down after he went down below. He may be still down there or in the sleeping room. He could be asleep, too. There's not much to do here in the dark," she said, yawning.

"I'll go see if he's in the back room," said Adam.

"Let's all go in," said Mabon. "We can turn on the lights. But don't touch that switch, Adam, until the bedroom door is shut tight."

Adam, who was ahead of the others, made his way to the door, and, once Blanchfleur had risen to her feet, they all followed. At the door he stopped and held it wide for the others. "I'm not staying," he said, "unless there's some food. I'm too tired."

No one questioned him or offered food. He walked out to the sofa, where he found Lucky curled up on one end, already asleep.

Ueland had heard the commotion from the bedroom after being awakened by Lucky's sharp bark. He was standing by the bed as the door was closed firmly and the light came on in the windowless room. Everyone blinked at the sudden harsh light.

"It looks like everyone's arrived safe and sound," Ueland said. "How was your short journey?"

"Short?" said Tish, offended. "It seemed long enough to me. It was hard walking so far, carrying all that stuff."

"Yes," said Alice. "Even though it seemed like we left almost everything we owned behind."

"The trip went smoothly and we have no bad incidents to report," said Mabon.

"So nothing going on out there at all?" said Doctor Ueland. He stepped to the sink and began to fill the kettle.

Nora spoke then. "We saw a lot more helicopters not so long ago. Thankfully they didn't see us."

"Helicopters...how many?" asked Ueland, his voice tight and angry.

"Maybe a dozen. Troop carriers," said Mabon.

"Heading south?" Ueland continued.

Mabon nodded.

The doctor sighed. "They must mean to do a further

clean-up operation in the area where the workers got out of the tunnels. We can only hope they haven't found all the exits and the men have had time to disperse widely. I hoped perhaps the Federation would leave a few of them alone to live out what was left of their time. They couldn't pose a threat to insiders. Their days are certainly numbered."

"What do you mean, numbered?" Tish asked. "Are they all going to get killed?"

Alice answered. "They can't ever have children of their own. They are workers and they have no work and no place to live," she said.

"Then why kill them?" Tish asked.

"The Federation leaders are very angry at me and all I did against their will in and around Aahimsa," said Blanchfleur. "They say they are afraid of the threats from the past like we all were. But they have become fanatics about it. They want a final end to the old world of men. And men themselves."

"Will they hurt us?" Tish asked her grandmother. "Is that why we're running away? I heard Nora say they might want to kill all of us."

"Do you really believe that, Nora?" asked Blanchfleur.

"Yes, I do. I don't think they'll intentionally set out to kill Tish or Alice. But if they try to capture and dispose of us, who knows what will happen?" said Nora. "They've killed lots of women in the past. Don't get fooled that because they're female they can't be as dangerous as males. Surely you of all people know that."

"Let's hope we never find out what they'll do," said Blanchfleur. "And," she said looking sternly at Nora, "let's try and not frighten the children any more than we have to."

"With all that military hardware outside," interrupted Ueland, "I suggest we all stick together and from now on travel underground as long as that is possible. It appears to be the safest alternative. Blanchfleur and I found the trip through the tunnel quick and effortless, verging on pleasant."

At this point the conversation was interrupted by a powerful distant explosion. Moments later the ground shook enough that dishes in the cupboards rattled for several long seconds and everyone became instantly frightened. No one spoke for a moment. Ueland picked up his things and made his way toward the door.

"Grab what you can of your belongings and follow me," he said, then turned off the light and hurried toward the downstairs exit. Everyone struggled in the dark to pick up their things and followed him down the stairs. Mabon came last and hurriedly closed the door and heard the lock click shut in the darkness of the staircase.

The generator was still humming along and Ueland flicked on a small light near the exit. Mabon saw that two small service vehicles sat at the ready, their headlamps lighting the gloomy tunnel ahead of them.

"Who will operate the first car?" asked Nora.

"I showed Blanchfleur the ropes on the way here. She learns fast, which came as no surprise to me. She'll teach her passengers and I'll teach mine," said Ueland. "By my estimation we now have four fully charged batteries and enough power to run for twelve hours in total without charging them again. The plan is to get to the distant station down near where the north end of the lake flows out into a long river that runs to the east of the continent.

"As far as the Federation and I know, the area around that station is totally uninhabited. If we set out from there we should be out of sight from the eyes in the sky. We should be able to go anywhere, to travel until we find a spot where we can build a shelter for the winter and find a way to feed and care for one another.

"Now, no more talk. Get aboard one or the other with your gear. Let's get going. I believe they blew up the service building we left earlier and perhaps they'll blow this one soon, or all of them; who can know these things. Hurry!" He entered the service room and cut the engine to the power generator. The emergency lights were operating on reserved battery power.

"Of course, it's up to any and all of you whether you want to come with us," said Ueland,

"How long will it take to get where we're going?" asked Tish.

"Now that depends," said Ueland. "I would prefer one long day's travel. It will be tiring and highly boring, especially to the youngsters."

"How long if we go directly?" Mabon asked.

"I would guess, that if nothing goes wrong, we should get there in less than five hours."

"Five hours," said Tish. "Great Goddess. I don't think I can stand it."

"I'm basing it on travelling about thirty kilometres per hour," Ueland said.

"Will the carts go any faster?" asked Alice.

"Yes, a bit faster. But thirty is fast enough if we have to stop suddenly."

"Why would we have to stop suddenly?" asked Alice.

"I don't know," said Ueland. "There could be anything or anyone out there, or some animal. We don't want a crash."

Adam had been watching everyone's faces. He could see that Blanchfleur was growing impatient. She listened to Ueland deliver his decisive responses, so self-assured, and somehow it was annoying her. She wasn't used to playing second fiddle to anyone.

She stood and turned to Ueland. "Will I be driving the lead car?" she asked.

"If you wish," he answered.

"Then can I use my judgement as to the speed?"

"I suppose that makes sense."

No one had time to complain or protest or object to who would pilot them away from their comfortable sanctuary. No one seemed to care.

Adam was surprised when Blanchfleur suggested that Alice and Nora and Tish travel up front with her if no one minded. That would leave Mabon and Ueland and Adam and Lucky to follow in the second car.

"It might be nice," she said, "if I could have some female company." Adam noticed that the mayor hadn't said "insider" company. He guessed she was very aware that they were all outsiders now. He asked Mabon if he minded Nora travelling with Alice, who used to be her special friend.

"No, I'm glad to have some time with all the men, with

you and Ueland and Lucky," his dad said with a chuckle.

"But will you miss Mom. I missed her and you when I was at the Manuhome...but that was for a long time. I used to cry at night when no one could hear me. But I got used to missing both of you. I'm glad we're together again." He pressed himself against his father and then, embarrassed, punched him on his solid shoulder.

Mabon smiled and tapped him very gently on the chin with his massive fist. "I miss her," he said, "every minute she's away from me."

Blanchfleur and Ueland had a short meeting just before they finished loading the gear and checking that the batteries were properly stowed aboard.

"How far should I go before I stop?" Blanchfleur asked.

"How about two hours?" Ueland suggested. "Then we'll stop and assess things. We'll stop at the station nearest to the two-hour point, okay?"

"How will I know what time it is?"

He took out his pocket watch and unfastened the chain from his belt loop. "Here," he said, handing it to her with a smile.

Blanchfleur headed for her cart, watch in hand, with Nora and Alice and Tish following behind. Adam waited until they were all aboard before he climbed onto the second car with Lucky and the men.

Alice sat beside her mother and Tish sat behind her. Nora sat behind Blanchfleur. She found herself uncomfortable, and though she knew it was unreasonable, felt a little disloyal to Mabon and Adam. She nearly asked to be allowed to go to the cart behind them, but Blanchfleur wasted no time in getting started. She pushed the throttle forward and they were soon travelling ahead in the dim light at a brisk clip. The car bumped and lurched enough that she slowed to a speed that seemed much more manageable.

Nora noticed that Tish had been watching her closely. The eleven-year-old was such a pretty thing, this miniature Alice. Nora remembered the day they went picking blueberries. Alice had been so beautiful, so young. She'd probably looked exactly like Tish when she was eleven. It would be so easy to like this little girl. She seemed so much like Alice used to be at her kindest, her most thoughtful.

Nora smiled at Tish, and then watched the tunnel flashing hypnotically past in the space between Alice and her mother and to either side. She watched for a few minutes, although there was little of interest to see. She noticed before long that Tish was watching her again. Nora smiled kindly at the girl and this time, timidly, the child smiled back.

"You used to like my mother, didn't you?" Tish asked, looking into Nora's eyes.

"Yes," she said, after a moment's hesitation. "We were very fond of one another."

"And you left because of the baby," Tish said. The girl turned and looked back at Adam, who sat in the front of the car behind them next to Ueland. "Are you glad you ran away?"

"Hush," said Alice. "Don't be impertinent." Nonetheless she waited, interested in the answer if it should come.

Nora hesitated. She had no interest in coming between the girl and her family. "It wasn't easy at first, but I'm glad

Adam is alive and here with us today."

"Were you scared?" Tish continued. "I'd be too scared to do something like that."

"I was very scared. I thought we were both going to die. But we didn't. And, yes, I'm glad I ran away. But I was sad that I hurt your mother and made your grandmother angry. And I'm sad that all those people had to die."

Nora tried not to cry, but tears welled up and ran down her face, though she managed to weep briefly in silence. Her mind carried her back to Aesop and Brin and the old ones and to the many Rangers who died in the battles because they were Blanchfleur's slaves and they were powerless to resist.

Nora knew that Alice and Blanchfleur must have heard the conversation behind them, but they gave no sign of it.

Tish looked at Nora with a sad expression on her lovely young face. Nora noted the dampness around the child's eyes that glistened in the dim light provided by the headlights of the car following them. "I'm sorry," she said quietly, as if it were something she herself had done.

Tish looked away again, but a while later she looked at Nora once more with a wondering stare. "What is it?" Nora asked.

"Was it scary living with the big Ranger? Were he and the outsider boy dangerous? Did they ever hurt you?" Tish said, then looked down toward the floor of the car.

Nora reached and touched her gently on the arm. The girl looked up at her, embarrassed.

"It was never difficult living with him. He is the gentlest person I've ever known, and the sweetest. Adam is his equal. They were only dangerous to those who threatened us, they never hurt me, ever."

"Would they hurt me or my family?"

"No, they will only help you and your family."

"But my family tried to hurt you," said Tish.

"We know...and that time is over. We will never hurt one another again," said Nora as she and Tish looked with open hearts and minds deeply into one another's eyes. Tish turned and looked back at Adam beside Ueland and smiled. The boy waved and smiled back. He looked surprised and pleased. She felt much safer now than any time since the final morning she awoke in Aahimsa.

Chapter 17: In the Car Behind

Adam was gently rubbing Lucky's ears. The old dog had slept for the first part of the dark journey in spite of the slight, irregular bumps when the wheels met seams in the rails beneath them, but now he was awake and restless. He whined from time to time as the walls of the tunnel slid eerily past. Adam wondered how much better the dog could see than the rest of them. Adam focused on the car ahead of them, since it received most of the benefit of their service car's tiny headlights. Still, he glanced around enough to see that they had passed at least three service buildings.

As he stared at the rear of the car ahead he noticed that his mother and the girl, Tish, were busy talking to one another and Tish had glanced back more than once toward his car. One of those times she actually seemed to smile at him. He was happy that she may not be as afraid of him and Mabon and even Doctor Ueland as she used to be.

"The girl smiled at us," he said to Mabon, who sat behind Ueland, who was handling the speed control and had one foot always on the brakes. Ueland's eyes seldom left the track or the car ahead. He maintained a small distance between them.

"I noticed," said Ueland. "I expect she was smiling at you, however. She has never shown much interest in me. Why would she? To her I'm an old work beast. Tish and her mother have always maintained a respectable distance between themselves and me."

"But you and Blanchfleur are friends," Adam said. "I don't get that."

"What don't you get?" asked Ueland, concentrating on his driving.

"How you could trick her about the old ones and about us and still be friends with her? She had the power to punish you, or even kill you, and she didn't ever."

"We aren't exactly friends," the doctor said. "We worked together for many years building the Manuhome. She trained me and proposed all the major plans. She set up the business and managed the trade and distribution of product and goods manufactured. I figured out how to implement and develop what we manufactured and grew. We made a pretty good team. I guess you'd say we have mutual respect, so perhaps that's why we care what happens to each other."

Adam said nothing, satisfied for the moment, though he suspected Ueland wasn't telling him the whole story.

"Do you think Blanchfleur cares about anybody but herself?" asked Mabon from his seat behind them. He had been following the conversation with considerable interest.

"Yes, a bit too much sometimes. She was the one in charge of everything and everyone. When you're in charge in this world, you do what you have to do, or else. I'm sure that shooting arrows at Rangers and setting them on fire wasn't something you'd always dreamed of doing. When we get backed into a corner by violence we fight back, or we die and let our friends and loved ones die," said Ueland.

"So you're saying we're as bad as she is?" said Mabon, a bit annoyed.

"No, I'm saying no such thing. You were trying to save your family's lives and those of your friends. She was trying to save her city and protect her assets. Of course, she may have been thinking of her family and the lives of her workers. I'm just saying that things are never simple. Blanchfleur didn't invent the city-states, but she was an important part of the system. We're all born into systems and situations. We start off where we land, and we do what we think is best, even the worst and the most unprincipled of us."

"So you're protecting Blanchfleur?" said Mabon.

"I'm protecting all of us, in case you haven't noticed," said Ueland, his voice gruff and impatient and showing more emotion than usual.

"Yes, but why her?" continued Mabon relentlessly.

"Why not? I have various reasons for protecting all of you," said Ueland, smiling at Adam and turning back to face Mabon.

"What reasons?" asked Adam as he glanced toward the car ahead of them. "Look out!" he shouted, his shrill voice joining the screams from the voices and the braking steel wheels of both vehicles.

Ueland had pushed hard enough on the brakes that they stopped just short of the rear bumper of Blanchfleur's service vehicle. Ueland turned off the electric motor of their car and jumped down to the rail bed, followed by Adam and Mabon and the dog. They hurried past the front car and Ueland shone his pocket flashlight at the huge, dark mass that almost completely blocked the tunnel ahead of them.

Adam glanced toward his mother, Tish, and Blanchfleur, who sat staring open-mouthed at the back end of what he now saw was a large passenger rail car blocking the rails dead ahead of them. They had come pretty close to being part of a serious accident. He bent down to try and silence Lucky, who had begun to growl and bark at the rear of the darkened car. He drew the dog close and patted him as he spoke quietly until the old dog settled, still occasionally whining.

"Come with me, Mabon," said Ueland as he stepped

toward the massive train car that blocked their way.

"I'll go too," said Nora, and Blanchfleur and the others followed her cautiously, not knowing what to expect.

"I don't get this," said the mayor as she caught up to Ueland. "Did you know about this railcar? This rail line hasn't been fully operational for over three years. There has been nothing scheduled to go this way since we permanently shut down the holiday excursions to the River Islands. It's only been used for special, official traffic that was under my control, or so I thought."

"No, this rig is as much a surprise to me as to you. My maintenance workers have serviced the buildings and the rails for occasional or emergency use as we were instructed, but the line hasn't been authorized for any other use that I know of." Ueland left them and walked up to the car, standing next to the steps leading to the rear platform.

He gestured to Mabon and Adam, who climbed the metal steps onto the rear platform, where they found the door locked tight. "Do you have a key for this?" asked Adam as he turned toward Ueland. The doctor reached into his pocket and tossed his ring of keys to Adam.

"Second short brass key to the right of the leather tab," said Ueland. Adam held the ring up against the lights from Blanchfleur's car and quickly found the key, then opened the door, which swung easily on its hinges.

"Check it out," said Ueland.

Mabon and Adam entered cautiously and then all climbed aboard and pressed inside the upholstered interior. They huddled together and looked nervously here and there about the dark car, not knowing what to expect.

Adam flicked a wall switch out of curiosity, and to his great surprise, the overhead fluorescents flickered on. As they walked through the car between the seats, the others looked into overhead storage compartments, and into the small washroom at the end. The toilet still held remarkably clean water.

"This carriage must have left Aahimsa just before we did," Ueland said. "I wonder who was aboard and where they are now."

"I wonder," said Blanchfleur. "I wonder —" Her face showed that she was worried and thinking she might know who was involved.

"What is this?" asked Nora, pointing to her right. She stopped beside one of the seats and dug around until she discovered a single apple jammed halfway down between two of the plush, comfortable seats. The shiny red fruit was still looking quite edible. It couldn't have been there too long or it would have spoiled. She handed the sweet-smelling globe to Blanchfleur. The mayor looked at it and handed it back to Nora.

"Perhaps one of the youngsters would like it. It's still hard and cool," said Blanchfleur. "So, obviously someone fled the city immediately before the attack. Perhaps they had the means to know it was coming. We will have to be even more vigilant from here on in. They must be around here someplace or not far up ahead. They may indeed be armed and dangerous. But at least they're not robots. It's easier to deal with people than robots."

"How do you know they're not robots?" asked Tish, staring at her grandmother.

Blanchfleur tousled her hair and smiled warmly. “Robots don’t eat apples, do they?”

Mabon cleared his throat. Nora looked at him. “What?” Nora said.

Mabon hesitated. He caught Nora’s eyes and she smiled her encouragement. He cleared his throat again. “Could they have been picked up by one of those helicopters?”

Blanchfleur nodded. “Of course, you’re right. Some or all of them may have been. But it would be a long walk to Aahimsa from here. More likely, they may be up ahead or back in any of the service buildings we passed today. We don’t know who they are or what they stand for. We can’t assume they are enemies or friends, dangerous or helpful. But they may indeed be hostile to us and we must prepare to treat them as such. Even if they mean us no harm, they can still intentionally or accidentally report our presence to the Federation. That would be dangerous or perhaps fatal for more than one of us.”

“I wonder why they stopped right here?” Tish asked.

No one had seen Ueland enter the car from outside. “Cave-in,” he said. “Up ahead. Part of the ceiling is down; there’s a large boulder in between the tracks. Perhaps shaken down by one of the explosions.”

“Is the train wrecked?” Adam asked Ueland.

Mabon put his arm across the boy’s shoulder and held him close. Nora watched her two men with pride, and awaited Ueland’s answer.

“I don’t think so,” said Ueland. “I couldn’t see much with this small light. But I could tell that several people with small shoes had been working for some time to clean up the mess and move the stone. It was pretty large and they either failed or just gave up in frustration."

"I bet we could do it if we all worked hard," said Adam.

"Can we get the train going again if we can clean up the mess?" asked Blanchfleur. "Are the tracks badly damaged?"

"There is still plenty of power in the batteries and there's a small gasoline engine and generator that would take us easily to the next service building where we could quickly give it a full charge. And there are the batteries from both of our service cars. And, no, I don't think the tracks are all that seriously damaged. I think we can move the boulder, in spite of its size, and clear things up if we all pull together."

"Why don't we just continue in the cars we've been using?" asked Tish.

"It would be a major task to get them past this train," said Ueland. "There are six full-size cars up ahead, and the engine. Those service cars are mostly iron and steel, not something we could lift or carry, and seven cars' distance is a long way to move them even if we could."

"So there could have been a big crowd aboard," said Blanchfleur.

"Anywhere from a handful to several hundred if they squeezed in," said Ueland. "My guess is that was a last-minute decision, so perhaps we're talking a small group of traitors who were caught off guard by the attack — some of your own people who favoured the Federation's politics."

"You may be right," the mayor said. "There were more than a few of them."

Mabon approached and waited patiently, not wanting to interrupt. Ueland signalled for him to speak.

"We're ready to work," said Mabon, "Adam and Nora and I."

"Let's get at it," said Blanchfleur. "I'll get the others organized."

"We'll get all the gear we can find aboard the storage compartments of the engine and the cars and set up the lights," said Ueland. He led the three former residents of the Happy Valley through the train toward the front, stopping by each car and picking up as many tools as they could carry.

Chapter 18: A Good Night's Sleep

A few hours later, the rock had been rolled to the side with the help of two lengths of I-beam steel, from the broken ceiling, used as a pry. Mabon used his great strength to transfer the heavy reserve batteries from the service vehicles while others repaired and reinforced one of the damaged rail ties and moved hundreds of smaller rocks and debris.

Ueland and Mabon rigged up the two spare batteries and connected them to the train's power system, Mabon supplying the brawn and Ueland his skill and knowledge. Then the two men, with the assistance of Nora and Blanchfleur, disconnected the final four cars while Adam and Tish and her mother looked on.

Then everyone climbed aboard and waited nervously while Ueland and Mabon started the engine and slowly and carefully towed the two front cars of the train past the crudely repaired site of the cave-in. Then they walked back together to the site of the cave-in to drag the boulder far enough back across the rails to block the track, preventing anyone from pursuing them easily via this route.

After a very short conversation where the men suggested they get going, and the older of the women reminded the men of everyone's fatigue, they unanimously decided to catch some sleep in the relative safety and comfort of the stationary train before setting off into the darkness ahead.

Ueland and Blanchfleur showed the others how to make up the seats into relatively comfortable beds, complete with small pillows. Tish and Adam were delighted with the apple and were quick to insist on keeping it so they could eat it later.

"Put it in your jacket pocket," Tish said. "Don't you dare eat it."

Adam nodded, happy to be carrying the apple. He would take good care of it. The others snacked on crackers and peanut butter from the bag of items taken from the service building they had last visited.

"Where are we going tomorrow?" asked Tish.

"Let's talk in the morning," said Alice. "Let's just dream of better days ahead as we try and get some sleep while we're exhausted and somewhat relaxed."

"Well put, Alice," said Ueland. "We can talk as we zip along in the morning. Make sure everyone has loaded all of their things aboard. You may very well wake up to find the train moving swiftly along."

"Would anyone mind if the insiders sleep in the rear car and the outsiders in the front one?" suggested Alice.

"Sleep where you want," said Nora, "but I intend to be with Mabon and Adam, even if it means sleeping in the engine car."

"There's no need for that," said Blanchfleur. "We're all outsiders now, I believe. I'll be sleeping in my clothes. If anyone wants to change there is the toilet compartment. I suggest sleeping wherever you feel most comfortable. This could be the last day of comfort for a while. We may have enemies ahead who wish us evil."

Nora shot her a warning glance and pointed to the young ones. "That, too, can be a topic of conversation for the morning. So, goodnight!"

"I suggest we adults talk for a few minutes now," Mabon said to Nora, just loudly enough that Blanchfleur and Ueland heard.

Ueland indicated with a nod of his head that they should follow him and they did. Adam had been listening and he followed as well. As they passed Tish and her mother, they rose from their half-made beds and followed. They arrived in the small control cabin of the engine car. Blanchfleur noticed the youngsters.

"You two kids should get back to bed," she said and stood there with her arms crossed, looking firm.

Adam spoke quickly. "I'm staying."

Blanchfleur looked toward Nora and Mabon, who turned to one another and simultaneously shrugged. "Adam more than took care of himself during the attack in the valley," said Nora. "He can stay."

"What about Tish and Alice?" asked the mayor, suddenly unsure of herself and doing her best to appear conciliatory.

"I'm staying, Mother," said Alice. "I would prefer to know what's going on."

"Me, too," said Tish. She wanted very much to stay near the adults she knew and relied on.

"You may not like what you hear, darling," said Blanchfleur. "I'm going to leave it up to your mother."

"I'm staying," said Tish emphatically. Alice shrugged.

"Let her stay," said Adam. "She's a person, too." If he could stay, why shouldn't she? Besides, it was nice to have another kid around, even if she was an insider.

Tish looked at Adam with an expression he couldn't read, an odd mixture of appreciation and resentment. That look bothered him a bit, made him feel awkward and uncomfortable, but he still wanted her to stay.

"Okay, let's talk," Mabon said. "Blanchfleur, you seem to have some clear ideas of what we might find up ahead. So do I and so do the others, I imagine. I'd like to hear your thoughts and whatever solutions you might have. For instance, I'm wondering if it might make sense to travel in the deep of the night, when most people will choose to be asleep. Our enemies will probably go to the undamaged service centres or to some camping area for the night. The planes and the satellites and the robot drones will be looking for light or sound, but we'll be underground. We can slow down as we pass the service buildings. That sort of thing."

"That makes sense, regarding the human enemies, at least. The drones and the kill bots don't care about the time of day or about light or dark, but some of their controllers do," said Blanchfleur, as she ran her long fingers through her hair, trying to shake out some of the dirt and untangle the many knots the day's activities had brought to it. "I expect that we may find some of the traitors somewhere up ahead.'

"It would be my guess that they were duped into betraying Aahimsa and they discovered too late that their treachery would not be rewarded except by termination by Federation forces. Perhaps they've all been apprehended by the Federation, but I expect not. There weren't any signs of a violent attack against the train."

"What sort of weapons can we expect them to have?" asked Mabon.

"I assume you refer to the train passengers," said Blanchfleur. "If you are thinking of them as citizens who betrayed us, there may be members of the police with them. If so they could have powerful Tasers; if not, I can't be sure. There was little need for weapons in Aahimsa. But we can't know for sure."

"You think they could be someone else?" asked Nora, her green eyes alert and worried.

"Anything is possible," said Blanchfleur, turning her dark

eyes on Ueland. "Possibly some of your workers, Doctor."

"Not likely," he said. "My workers were hit first during the attack, which began at the Agrihome. The ones who did escape were headed through tunnels running south and west. They would never risk entering the city."

"What about Federation fighters?" asked Alice.

"Yes," said Blanchfleur. "This is a real worry. There were rumblings lately of unauthorized visitors from the Federation arriving unannounced and speaking at various gatherings in Aahimsa. If some of these were professional fighters, they'll have access to some of the most powerful weapons on the planet."

"But there may be nobody at all up ahead. So what do you propose we do?" asked Mabon, his arms crossed and his jaw set firmly.

"And where should we head?" asked Nora, moving over near Mabon, who uncrossed his arms and pulled her gently close to him, his jaw relaxing. "Should we get out of this tunnel and travel over land somewhere?"

Ueland stepped into the conversation. "We should head for Queenstown. Blanchfleur has suggested to me that there are a couple of excellent places nearby where we could hide for a while until the situation cools off. And if not somewhere in the city ruins, there are the offshore islands and all the abandoned land across the river and along the other side of the lake. It sounds like an excellent starting place with lots of options."

"One person with a mobile phone or a single light can let the Federation know we're here," said Adam. "Wouldn't it be better to avoid any place where people might gather?"

"Yes, without a doubt. That would be real trouble," said Mabon. "Look what they've done to Aahimsa and the Manuhome."

After a bit of conversation and assurance from Blanchfleur that one unknown location was as dangerous as another, and that Queenstown offered, in her opinion, the best available possibilities for safe haven, they decided to stay with the train until Queenstown.

Afterwards, Adam and Tish were sitting on different ends of a bench along the back wall of the engine car. He turned and glanced at her. She noticed and turned angrily to him.

"What are you looking at?" she said.

"Sorry," said Adam, with a broad grin. "But I noticed you were looking at me a whole lot earlier."

"I never saw a young outsider before," she said, staring down at her dirty shoes and stockings.

"I never even saw another kid my age before," said Adam, laughing and feeling like he might have won the little game they were playing. "I only saw a few older kids working in the Manuhome, and I never was allowed to talk to them or be near them. And they weren't even allowed to talk to me or anything."

"Oh," she said, feeling a pang of sympathy. "I forgot about that."

"Your grandmother says we're all outsiders now. But you and I are the only kids," said Adam.

"But you'll always be the outsider to me," said Tish, feeling the need to separate herself from Adam.

"No, that's not true. I'm just a boy and you're just a girl. You'll be a woman and I'll be a man and we'll always be outsiders, both of us. Maybe we'll even be friends someday." He looked down at his badly scuffed and worn leather boots.

"Maybe we won't," she said, looking away again.

"I bet we will," he said cheerfully. He stood up and went out of the engine car.

Chapter 19: Heading for Queenstown

That night on the train, once everyone was settled for the night, Blanchfleur departed from the rear car where Alice and Tish lay curled up on two of the seats, already asleep. She joined Nora, Mabon, and Adam in the front passenger car. She found them sitting in silence and wide awake.

"Where's Ueland?" she asked and took a seat behind them.

"Up front in the engine car," said Adam. "Mabon is going to go up to join him in a minute. He thinks the doctor may need a break."

"Does anyone mind if I sleep here?" she asked, pointing at one of the empty seats.

"If you want," said Adam.

"Okay," said Nora, and Mabon said with a smile, "Fill your boots."

"Great," Blanchfleur said. "But before that, I'm going up with Ueland now, too, if you don't mind, Mabon. You coming?" she said, looking at Nora and Adam. They shook their heads and the other two went out the door one after the other.

After they left, Nora said to Adam, "You ready to sleep?"

"I'll try," he said. He moved close to her and she drew in so he could lean against her. He made no protest this time and Nora supposed it was because for the moment they were alone in the car.

"I saw you talking to Tish," said Nora.

"Yeah," he said, his voice already drowsy.

"What did she say?" she asked.

"Nothing much really. She says I'll always be an outsider," he said, yawning sleepily.

"What did you say?"

"I said we'd be friends someday."

"Good for you," she said. "I bet you'll be fine friends one day."

"Maybe," he said. "Probably. Goodnight, Mom. I love you."

Chapter 20: Somewhere Near Queenstown

When Adam next woke, the train was in darkness and perfectly silent. There was no sense of motion, no electric whirr from the engine. He slipped from under the sleeping bag that his mother must have drawn over him while he slept and fumbled his way to where he guessed the door to the engine room would be. He was relieved when, still half-asleep, he found it and entered the engine car. It was pitch black inside and completely empty.

Carefully, he made his way back to his sleeping bag and

crawled back inside. He wondered where everyone was but not for long as he was so groggy that he fell quickly back asleep. At some point he had a dream that came from time to time. He was back inside the valley where he and Nora and Mabon lived with the old ones who had managed to escape the Manuhome and carved out a few years of happiness for themselves. They took in Nora and Mabon and gave Adam the best years of his life. He learned from Nora and her books and the kindness and wisdom of Mabon. He learned love and courage and many skills from his adoptive parents and many skills from the old ones. The dream always ended with the battle, a hollow victory, and the sacrifices and deaths of the old ones. And then he startled and was awake.

"Queenstown," Adam heard someone say aloud. Someone had turned on a small light in the car and most of the others were up and dressed for the day and gathered together around the rear section. He shook the confusion out of his drowsy head and sat up quickly.

"You're awake," a voice said from the seats opposite him. He turned and saw Tish there, squatting on the seat opposite him. "We're stopped somewhere under that Queenstown place," she said.

"We're here," he said, "and we're safe."

"Maybe," she whispered. "I don't really feel safe. I'm a bit scared."

"What have they been saying?" he asked and handed her the apple he'd been carrying since they got on the train. She held it high in her hand. "Give it back and I'll divide it," he said.

"All I heard was my grandmother telling someone what I told you. Then they went to the back of the car and started talking quieter," Tish answered. She bit into the apple and handed it to him. "Have a bite," she said. "I guess if we have to be friends we can eat the same apple."

"Let's go up closer so we can hear," he said, taking the apple and biting into it. He handed it back to Tish. He had slept in his clothes and only took a moment to quickly fold and tie up his sleeping bag.

Tish held the apple and led the way. When they were close enough to hear the adults, they sat on opposite sides, keeping the aisle between them, handing the apple back and forth until it was gone save for the seeds and the crispy bits inside. Adam looked for someplace to put the damp bits he still held in his hand and finally dropped them into his shirt pocket.

Blanchfleur was speaking to the others and she paused to glance at the two youngsters briefly before continuing. "So today you will learn something about your options," she said, then pulled back her grubby hair, forming a ponytail that she fixed with a heavy rubber band. She appeared to Adam to have become somehow younger and softer during their travels. He guessed that it was only from getting to know her a bit more.

"What is there to learn, Mom?" asked Alice, who seemed brighter and more relaxed this morning, too. "We're in the wild and there's really no perfectly safe place we can go, is there?"

"Time will tell," her mother said, her face hopeful. "There are no completely safe places. Good times come and go no matter where you are."

"Have you been keeping secrets from us?" asked Ueland with a teasing grin.

"You aren't the only one with secrets," the mayor said. "We all have lots of untold stories to tell, don't we, Ueland?"

"Yes, that's true," he said. "Are we going to tell all now?" he asked. He was enjoying himself, as was Blanchfleur.

"No, not all of them. But I'm going to explain something that will surprise a few of you, perhaps all of you. It may prove helpful to us or may prove to be a problem or something in between. But bear with me and you will hear some of it.

"As mayor of Aahimsa, I had a certain amount of power to shape the futures of many people. There were, however, certain lines drawn in the sand that I crossed not only at my peril but also to the endangerment of my entire city and its population along with its attachments and enterprises."

"Like the Manuhome?" said Mabon, his voice low and sad.

"Exactly," she said. "Like the Manuhome."

"And what about the Happy Valley?" asked Adam, wondering if he had said too much.

Blanchfleur hesitated, momentarily annoyed. Then she gathered herself together and smiled. "Yes, like the valley."

"But you didn't know anything about the old ones' valley for a long, long time," said Nora.

"Don't be too sure," said Ueland.

"What do you mean?" asked Alice, raising her voice.

"I'm sorry, but we don't have time for this now," said Blanchfleur. "If things work out we will have time for all of these questions before long. If not, they won't matter anyway. All that matters for the moment is getting us all to a safe place."

"Where is this safe place?" asked Mabon, moving closer.

"If it hasn't been destroyed like all the other places that we used to love, it is not far from where we are right now," she said.

"In Queenstown?" asked Tish.

"There is no 'Queenstown' as such," said Blanchfleur. "There is a place in what was once a small city above where we are located in the tunnel, in a partially destroyed set of buildings once used by a group of religious women from the old world. They called themselves 'sisters' and lived together in a community where they shared everything they had and worked and prayed together to help their community and serve their god."

"Did they have children?" asked Tish.

"They had no children of their own. They sometimes worked in schools as teachers of children or in hospitals serving others. It was other people they worked to serve and in that way and through their prayers they served their god. They lived simple lives together as individuals. I understand that they were quite happy, for the most part, doing that."

"Did they get married?" asked Adam. He had never heard of these people.

Blanchfleur laughed. "In a way, they did. This was long ago in the old world, long before the insider cities. They followed an outsider, a holy man they called Christ, whom they believed to be the Son of God. They believed this Son had come to earth and died for the sins of everyone and then was killed and returned to his father. These sisters would sometimes say they were the brides of this Christ."

"Do they still live here?" asked Tish.

"No, dear. That was many years in the past. They have all died and gone."

"Then where are we going and is there someone there?" asked Adam.

"That depends on whether the Federation knows about what I did here at this place, this ancient monastery where these women lived in community and followed a strict set of rules in common."

"What did you do?" asked Tish.

"Remember that the World Federation of City-States had many laws about what insiders could do and couldn't do." She looked from face to face and saw that everyone was waiting for the next words. "Well, there are always those who disagree and try to do things their own way without considering the consequences of their words and their actions, right, Nora? Nora can understand this."

Nora nodded. She was very aware of the consequences of her actions. Adam was here, close by and alive, to prove it, and she had no regrets about that.

"I have many regrets centred around all that followed, but I can't say I would have done, or, indeed, could have done anything different than I did," said Blanchfleur. "Nora's escape with Adam was an event I had no control over, and no say in. She chose to leave the protection of Aahimsa with a foundling child born outside our laws who had no rights to exist. I predicted her actions would have dire consequences and they did. We've all seen what happened to Aahimsa and the Manuhome once the Federation found its excuse to destroy us."

"So it's all my fault?" said Nora on the verge of tears.

"No, Nora, it is not your fault. Even if it was the consequences of your choice and the actions that followed. But it would likely have happened sooner or later. It may have happened at exactly the same time, or even earlier if you had not saved the child. You acted out of love and that is never anyone's fault. Ueland acted out of love when he tried to save the old ones. And I, too, acted out of love on several occasions. I am about to tell you of one of them."

"You acted out of love quite often," interrupted Ueland, his voice tender, not at all the official, controlled voice they were used to hearing from him.

"Not now, Doctor. Please, not now. Let me get on with this."

"Very well," said Ueland, "continue." He stepped back a few feet from where she stood.

"You haven't told us what you did," said Tish. "What you did when you acted out of love."

"I was very close to telling you my secrets, but that would have spoiled the fun. It would also have placed all of you in greater danger, so I've decided to show you rather than tell you about my foolish, headstrong act of love. You will have to wait until we arrive at our destination and settle in. I'm still not certain that our sanctuary awaits. I don't know how much the Federation knows about my activities. I've tried to keep them secret, but you all know how difficult it can be to keep those secrets.

"All I'll say for now is that I have defied the Federation in several ways over the years. Ueland knows some of these ways, but I don't think he knows about the existence and the extent of this one. But you'll know soon if all goes as planned. I have a feeling that you'll all be surprised and delighted at what I've done." Blanchfleur smiled and sat down a moment to rest.

"If the Federation hasn't found and destroyed the place, our hiding place should be waiting for us under the ruins of the old monastery nearby. We will try to visit later tonight if conditions allow."

Chapter 21: The Monastery

"When we travel out there in the open, we won't want to look like moving human beings to the eyes in the sky," said Mabon just before they set out into the darkness from the small service building on the outskirts of what had once been Queenstown. "We will want to look like individual wild animals or a pack of them, so we will spread out and move fairly quickly, varying our rates of speed. Watch what Lucky does and the way he moves."

Mabon knew, by the sparse light seeping in through the small windows in the long-unused building, that night had arrived on the outside, and if they showed no artificial light they should not be visible to the casual passage of the orbiting eyes. There was no reason for the Central Council to pay serious attention to this region. If everyone was careful they would be of no more interest than any of the creatures of the wild.

He had heard many stories from the old ones of the wild creatures living in the abandoned places far away from cities like Aahimsa. The wild outside Aahimsa that he and Nora had known as Adam grew to nine years of age would likely fill with more and more creatures as it reverted month after month to its more natural state now that it was no longer manipulated and exploited by humankind. Already he was imagining how they might live much as the old ones had in their hidden valley before the final attack of the Rangers that had been ordered by Blanchfleur, their fellow traveller. It pleased him, in a way, to imagine how he and Nora and Adam might show the city people how to live off the land, show them many of the skills they had been taught by the old ones.

Blanchfleur knew how to get to the monastery, which had been built into the side of a large hill constructed in a densely forested area in what had been Queenstown. It was close to where the original establishment had stood and had access to most of the lower floors and basement areas of that former building complex. She had visited regularly and brought along a few of Ueland's trusted engineers and builders to oversee the work. Ueland approved of their absence from the Manuhome but was never to be told the details of the work they had carried out in Queenstown.

These workers had been implanted with the same monitoring devices that had controlled the Rangers all those years without fail — except in the isolated case of Mabon, and that failure had been a freak accident due to Minn jumping to her death from the wall and accidently causing the cleaner to strike his neck against the jagged side of a metal wheelbarrow, extracting and destroying the device.

But Blanchfleur's last visit to the monastery had been a daytime event, when she was still in the good graces of the Central Council of the Federation and not a sought-after criminal. She wasn't used to managing a trip through the wild at night, so after providing the couple with a rough map, she had asked Mabon and Nora to lead the delegation on their outing to the monastery.

Lucky would travel with them, and Adam as well. When Tish learned that Adam and the dog were allowed to travel ahead of the others, she insisted on staying close to her grandmother. Originally she was to hang back with Alice underground, where she would be safe in case they encountered problems. After Tish insisted, Alice reluctantly agreed that they would all travel together — she had no intention of staying down in that dark tunnel all by herself.

Mabon offered everyone some of his bug repellent salve. Ueland, Adam, and Nora took dabs of it and applied it to face and neck and exposed skin. Blanchfleur took a bit and smelled it, then copied the others.

"I don't like this stuff," said Tish. "It stinks. Just like before. Will someone show me the right way to put it on?" She glanced over at Adam as Mabon extended the jar toward the youngster and she took a blob of paste on her finger. Adam lifted his finger and wiggled it, pretending to wipe paste on his palm and rub his hands together. He nodded at Tish, who rubbed her paste onto her hands. Adam pretended to rub his hands on his neck and then the rest of his exposed skin and Tish did the same. Reluctantly, Alice approached Mabon and took a dab for herself and carefully, with Tish's assistance, applied it like the others. Mabon put the jar away and they made their way outside.

The exterior air felt cool and clean and they tried to imitate wild animals as they moved, according to Mabon's instructions. Tish was excited by the brightness of the sky overhead and whispered to her mother and grandmother that they ought to look up. All paused to admire the amazing show of stars, moon, and planets overhead. Such a sight was impossible in the city, as artificial light extinguished most of the visible night sky.

As they stopped in their tracks, a few night insects found them and buzzed about their heads, but Mabon's salve seemed to stop them from landing and biting. Still, Blanchfleur and her family found their buzzing disturbing, and they were happy to get moving once again.

After what seemed a long trek crunching along a gravelled pathway that wound through a dense jumble of mixed hardwood trees, brush, and wild grasses, they came to a clearing where they found the remnants of several broken and fallen statues. The moonlight didn't allow enough light for them to properly inspect the shattered stone, but here and there were recently tended beds of fragrant flowers that contrasted with most of the wild tangle of green through which they passed.

"We're almost there," said Blanchfleur. "If you'll wait here, I'll make sure the path is safe and clear. Ueland will remain with you, and Mabon. Nora, if you'll be kind enough to join me, I'll be very pleased."

"Why me?" asked Nora.

"Politics, my dear. I don't want Adam and Mabon thinking I might be about to spring some nasty surprise on them. I want and need your complete trust. So come along and be a witness to all that passes. If my old friends are still here, I don't want to alarm them. They have survived this long by being wary of strangers. So we, too, must be wary for their sake."

The others watched as Blanchfleur led Nora toward the ruins of a large stone building. They stopped at a heavy wooden door and Blanchfleur pulled a key from her large black purse, inserted it in the lock, and opened it, and the unlikely companions disappeared inside, closing the door behind them.

"Is it all right if we stay real close together?" asked Tish, her voice frightened.

"If we're close enough we'll seem like a large animal," said Ueland. "Won't we, Mabon?"

"Perhaps."

Time passed slowly and the evening grew much cooler as clouds began to obscure the bright heavenly bodies overhead.

"Will they ever get back?" asked Alice after a long, nervous interval of standing in the deepening dark. And just then, as if in response, they heard a single set of footsteps approaching on the gravel path. They hardly dared breathe as Nora appeared out of the gloom.

"Come with me," said Nora.

"Who is in there?" asked Tish.

"You'll see," said Nora. "Blanchfleur is with them. She's been explaining everything to the ladies."

"Ladies?" said Tish.

"You'll see," said Nora, and she led them back in the direction she had come.

They followed silently, whispering nervously and brimming with curiosity.

Part 4

Chapter 22: The Meeting in the Monastery

They were greeted at the door by a very tall, elderly, deep-voiced woman with a generous grin who wore a dark grey, floor-length habit and black shiny leather boots with short flat heels that laced up the front. She wore a black cotton veil over a white starched linen coif that framed her large, moist, red face. On a black cord around her neck, made almost invisible by the black cotton veil, was suspended a silver cross that rested upon her matronly bosom. Her hands were fat and her fingers stubby and white as snow.

She worried a large set of clear glass prayer beads on a silver chain that hung from her belt. She lifted the silver cross on one end of the chain to her lips and kissed it as she smiled, bowed her head, and curtsied.

"We welcome our new friends to our sacred community," she said. "Come inside, please, and wait until I open the inside door. Then you'll meet the others."

The travellers entered the completely darkened space cautiously, huddling together in nervous silence.

"Have you properly closed the outer door?" asked the large woman.

"Yes," said Mabon. He felt awkward here in the darkness with this strangely dressed insider. He wondered where Blanchfleur had gotten herself to. He hoped everything was all right. Ueland had entered beside him and he felt Nora and Tish and Alice pressing close to him. Lucky also pressed close. Mabon could smell his dog's damp fur here in this warm, close, dark place.

The dog began to whine quietly and the insiders pressed even closer as the inside door was yanked open and all were temporarily blinded by the sudden intrusion of brilliant light breaking around the silhouette of the strange old woman who had welcomed them moments before.

Soon, though, they entered a large, comfortably furnished vestibule decorated by a variety of marble statues, some of which were of a young woman with a placid expression dressed somewhat like their greeter. The air was cooler and drier and smelled of fresh-cut flowers. There were other statues of a young bearded man dressed in like fashion and others of that same man suspended on a large cross, nails piercing his hands and feet, his bruised and bloodied head punctured by thorns.

Ueland recognized the images, and he knew this old woman represented something from the distant past. He knew about nuns and monasteries, and he knew about the old religions that had been traditionally practised by most of the people, or their ancestors, before the great transformation. This whole experience was startling, though. Blanchfleur had kept as many secrets from him as he had from her. He wondered if this whole religious sister thing was real or a cover-up. All could be revealed soon enough. Perhaps.

Everyone in his party was huddled closely together, already much more comfortable with one another, together in not knowing where they were going or what to expect when they got there. The old woman in her strange clothing stood at the far end of the room, where polished corridors, tiled in marble, led off in two directions.

"Are you all coming, then?" she asked.

"Who are you?" asked Alice.

"I am Sister Thomas of Providence," she said. "We are the Sisters of Providence. We are living out our lives here in the service of those who need our help and in the service of our Saviour." She paused. "But come along, please. The others will be curious and worried about what is keeping us. Blanchfleur is waiting with the sisters."

"Can Lucky come with us?" asked Adam. He had been looking around and taking everything in. *This is really weird,* he thought. But Adam had grown up living in what would have been a weird place to most of his new companions, surrounded by a group of strange old ones in a hidden valley. He hoped this would be another happy time. He waited for an answer from the big woman.

"And who is Lucky?" Sister Thomas asked with a knowing grin.

"Lucky is our dog," Adam said.

"Can you lead him over to me?"

"I'll try. He's really nervous of you," said Adam. He stepped toward the woman and said, "Come on, Lucky."

The dog hesitated but reluctantly followed. The old woman carefully bent enough to ruffle his greying ears. Lucky's tail began to wag as he licked the old woman's hand.

"We're friends already," said the old woman. "All friends who come in peace are welcome here. I hope we will all be good friends soon. Follow me, please." She began to walk down the hallway leading to the right and all followed in silence until they came to a door marked "Cloister. Silence Please. Out of bounds to all visitors."

Sister Thomas opened the door and, after herding people and dog into the dark space, threw a switch that clothed everything in darkness, then paused to close and lock the heavy metal door behind them. Lucky whined momentarily and then the lights came back on. They were now standing in a large room containing deep shelves of bedding and stacks of starched linen and dark shoes and stockings, and rows of black-and-white garments hanging from wooden hangers from suspended lengths of metal pipe.

"Come this way," Sister Thomas said as she slipped between rows of hanging black tunics and ducked under white cotton veils. Then she pushed something at eye level that caused a section of the back wall to slide to their right and allowed them to enter yet another large corridor. This one sloped gradually downwards. Once again she flicked switches and the room behind them darkened while the lights of the long corridor switched on and they began to walk swiftly behind Sister Thomas. They passed a couple of narrower corridors on their left and Lucky ventured a few metres down the next one they came to.

"Come, dog," Sister Thomas said, and Mabon ordered Lucky to come. Lucky knew enough to obey Mabon's voice. Adam was his best friend, but Mabon was the dominant force in his life, his first human friend, his clear master.

As Adam passed that corridor he wondered what Lucky had been attracted by down along that dark hall they had just passed. As the dog responded to Mabon's command, Adam thought he heard faint voices in the distance, young voices. He had never heard children playing, but what he heard was somewhat how he imagined the voices of children at play might sound. But children in this place...no, not possible.

Sister Thomas took the next corridor, this one to their right, and shut off the lights to the hall they had vacated. Next came a set of stairs that went down once again. The temperature had grown cooler as they descended, and so they were surprised to enter into an immense space rich with the smell of growing things and suffused with suffocating, moist heat. The room glowed under the bright, high ceiling.

As their eyes adjusted, they saw that they were standing inside a giant greenhouse. They recognized tall vines from which huge tomatoes were suspended, and all around them grew hundreds of flowers of many colours and varieties and plants of every description. A few dozen women dressed in a variety of tunics and robes worked at picking flowers and fruit and trimming vines.

So far they had seen no sign of Blanchfleur.

Sister Thomas clapped her hands firmly and all the young greenhouse workers stopped what they were doing, put down their gardening tools, and, picking up their full baskets, filed past the visitors and left the greenhouse. Sister Thomas followed and held the flimsy metal and glass door as the visitors, including Lucky, followed the young workers up one more corridor and into a large assembly hall. Sister Thomas stood with them until the workers took their seats, then directed the visitors up onto a small platform at the front of the hall, where Adam calculated there were more than enough chairs to hold them, facing the audience.

Adam took the time to let his eyes sweep across the hall and was astonished to realize that more than a hundred young women were there, most wearing the same clothing as Sister Thomas. Only the younger workers in front wore tunics that were less complicated and mostly white in colour. As he began to count the number of women in a single row and the number of rows to get a more exact number, Blanchfleur came out to join them, led by another elderly sister. He stopped counting and waited.

Sister Thomas allowed them a few moments to greet one another then gestured for all to take a seat. She went to the podium down front and was joined by the elderly nun who had brought Blanchfleur to the hall.

The meeting was pleasant and brief. Sister Thomas introduced Mother John the Baptist, who as it turned out was the Mother Superior of the Sisters of Providence. Mother John the Baptist welcomed everyone to the underground Queenstown Convent of the Sisters of Providence. She asked Mabon to stand, and then Ueland, and this prompted a polite round of applause. Adam came next and there was a much more vigorous and rousing round of applause and some gentle understated, nervous cheering. Nora brought polite applause, as well. She called Lucky, who stood on his hind legs, front legs on her shoulders, to lick her face, and introduced him. The nuns responded with happy laughter. When Blanchfleur was introduced and brought forward to the podium the house rang with sustained applause and cheering and the entire audience stood.

Nora and Mabon and Adam were amazed, as were Tish and Alice. Lucky simply barked loudly and excitedly. *This woman tried to kill us and was responsible for the deaths of the old ones,* Nora thought, *and these women are treating her like a hero.*

Mother Superior turned the meeting back over to Sister Thomas, who dismissed the audience, which returned once again to silence as they filed in an orderly manner out through the doors of the assembly hall. Sister Thomas turned to her guests and invited them to go with her.

Soon they were seated in a comfortably furnished lounge with soft chairs and a thick wool rug on the floor. They were served tea and sandwiches and, after a few minutes, Mother Superior returned. She and Sister Thomas announced that there would be time for questions and a discussion of future plans in light of a visit they had had a few days ago from another group of women who had been fleeing Aahimsa.

There had been five of them who, Blanchfleur figured, had been part of a larger conspiracy to hand the city over to the Federation, who had promised to implement a few simple changes that would bring Aahimsa in line with the other Federation cities. But once the raiders arrived and the defenses were breached, the attackers had turned on the "traitors" and executed more than half of them. These five visitors were part of a group who had barely escaped. One of the older sisters had met them outside the convent in full habit and had refused to speak to them as she was taking a solitary stroll under her vow of silence.

However, the frightened women told the silent, strolling sister of their plight, at first simply asking for help but then proceeding to threaten her, going as far as threatening to inform the Federation of the sister's presence here, an unauthorized person outside of city walls, and suggest to the Federation the possibility that there may be others of her kind living close by.

"Where are they now?" asked Blanchfleur, convinced she knew who at least one of these visitors would turn out to be. Few citizens of Aahimsa were ruthless enough to do what they had done to their sisters in their city. She knew who most of the leaders of her opposition were and she guessed they were capable of doing very stupid and short-sighted things. "Did the sister who met them catch any of their names?"

"I don't know. But I'll ask," said Sister Thomas. "I'm only glad we didn't let any of them inside. That would have been the end of everything we've accomplished here. There was something about them that alarmed the sister who encountered them outside. Once they began to threaten her she quickly gave them the slip."

"We'll have to be very careful about how we approach them, if, indeed, we ever do," said Blanchfleur.

Nora stood. She had plenty of questions, not least of which were the reasons behind the boisterous reception by the sisters, this large group of unauthorized outsiders. Why were they so glad to see Blanchfleur and her entourage? Still, Nora was pleased to discover these generous women. Their very existence warmed Nora's heart as it stirred so many memories of the old ones and the valley where she and Adam and Mabon spent so many happy years. But she had to know why they were so pleased to welcome all of them here.

"What's going on here? Do the sisters want something from us?" she asked the mayor when she got close enough to whisper without being heard. Blanchfleur had had a few short meetings to which Nora wasn't invited.

"Can I try to answer your question in the morning after breakfast?" she said. "I've been meeting with sisters Thomas and John and trying to get a clear picture of the situation while hearing their suggestions for our possible next steps. I'd hoped we could stay here for a bit, but if Gloria and her crowd of traitors are around here, the same ones who brought tragedy to Aahimsa — the sisters think they're in town here somewhere — there could be big trouble. I'll meet with the sisters again tonight. They can decide if they are willing to take the risk, and we can put all our cards on the table and let them know of all the risks involved, over breakfast. I promise you: no more secrets. Let's try and operate from a position of complete trust." She looked at Nora, realizing that Adam's mother had serious reservations about how ready she was to completely trust her former enemy. Blanchfleur hoped that what they all would hear from her in the morning would change all of that. But she knew that nothing she said to them was ever guaranteed to satisfy.

Chapter 23: No More Secrets

Their meeting was held in the cafeteria around two wooden tables that had been reserved for their use by the sisters. They had awoken and were dressed in time to arrive at eight, thinking they would be getting there in the midst of breakfast for the sisters. They were surprised to find the dining halls completely empty of people but filled with an abundance of food and drinks.

A chalkboard on an easel held a message in yellow chalk that welcomed them and informed them the nuns had finished morning prayers and were now at work. The note also advised them to help themselves to the food and then clean up. It became clear that the sisters did not eat meat of any kind but all were quite hungry and delighted to discover plenty of cereal and breads, cheeses, fried potatoes, delicious eggs in every possible style, and butter and baked goods galore, along with a good variety of fruit and vegetables.

Everyone ate happily from the delicious and bountiful larder. But greater than their hunger for food was their hunger for information, so they ate quickly and hurried to clean up in thoughtful silence. Then they gathered around their meeting tables and waited.

"Well?" Nora began, looking toward Blanchfleur, who rose.

"Before I begin," Blanchfleur said, "I would like to make one thing perfectly clear." She paused and looked at everyone in turn. "I am no longer the person in charge here. I would like you to consider who you would choose to be running the show when we eventually leave here."

"We were hoping you were about to tell us what is happening here in Queenstown. We were all under the impression that no one lived outside of the Federation cities," said Nora. There was a general murmur of agreement around the table.

"That sort of information will come in a moment. But first, it seems to me that Nora would make a fine leader, or perhaps she and Mabon with whoever agrees to help them. Before I tell you what you want to know, I need reassurance that all of us are together and that we will do our best to trust one another. After what has just happened to Aahimsa and finding out now that those who betrayed us may be close at hand, I'm a bit nervous about revealing what I know. Many more precious lives depend on our being loyal to one another. Can I trust all of you that you'll do nothing to harm those I am about to expose to your trustworthiness? I want to hear from each of you. Can I trust you? Answer yes or no." She pointed to everyone around the table. Each in turn, with a small bit of hesitation, answered yes.

"If the Federation discovers the existence of this convent, all the sisters, young and old, will probably die. Everyone they are protecting, including us, will likely not survive either. Do you all understand?"

"So how did this place survive outside the walls of Aahimsa?" asked Alice. "I understood that only those inside the cities and their workers were legally permitted to live after the great change."

"It's a long story that goes back initially before my time. This original convent did not survive. The religious sisters refused to come inside the walls. They were isolated until the oldest died and no others were permitted by law to join them. The convent lay empty for a long time afterwards."

"So where did these sisters come from?" asked Tish.

"Quite a few years ago, before I was mayor, my mother, who was the mayor back then, was informed by someone at the Federation that a covert group existed inside Aahimsa that was meeting regularly to discuss the possibilities of bringing back the old ways. They found the new ways difficult to accept. They wanted the right to give birth to sons as well as daughters and to bring them up to be non-violent.

"My mother was instructed by the World Council to turn them out of the city to face destruction by the Rangers or animals in the wild. She had to act on their orders or be removed as mayor. My mother knew if she were removed from office, her replacement would destroy everything she was in the process of accomplishing. Her mother had grown up in a small city called Kingston, which was near a large summer resort at that time popular with those of wealth in the city and which neighboured on the remains of an old monastery.

"Mother publicly turned those women out of the city, and, on the pretext of going on holiday, personally guided the group from a pre-arranged spot to safety in Kingston. Years later the mapmakers changed the name to Queenstown. The women were taken to the monastery and settled in. They were bored and began to read the books and papers of the nuns, and later they began to wear the clothes the long-departed sisters had worn. A number of years afterwards, when I had been elected mayor, I had my own rebellious group, a few young insiders who wanted to leave the city. I couldn't let them go unless I found somewhere to send them.

"I visited the old convent and to my surprise discovered that the new sisters were thriving and contented. They agreed to take the women in. In fact they were delighted to have possible new recruits. Since then I've sent many others. They have built wonderful lives for themselves. But if the Federation learns of this place, you can be sure all will be destroyed.

"There's more, and when you learn this you will be party

to information you may not wish to have. You may leave now if you wish to avoid becoming criminals in the eyes of the Federation. Once you hear this you will have no chance of turning back. You will also be carrying a heavy responsibility that could easily cost you your freedom and your life. So choose."

No one moved and Blanchfleur continued, "Several of those young insiders were with child when they left Aahimsa and came here."

"I heard them," said Adam, recalling the voices he thought he had heard on entering the convent. "I heard children when we were coming in here." There were gasps among the crowd.

"You may have indeed, Adam. There are a small number of children living among the sisters."

"Are any of them boys?" asked Tish, her voice nervous. There were more brief rumblings of conversation.

"There are some boys, although there are more girls. There are also a number of younger sisters who would leave here with their children if there were some place to go. They are hoping to get away before they are reported or discovered. And there is the matter of the traitor women from the city, who may yet be close by."

"It sounds like we have plans and choices to make," said Nora. "I think we should first deal with the traitors, as you call them. Do you think they're still around here? And are they a danger to us and the sisters even after what has happened?"

"Who can know for sure?" said Blanchfleur.

"Do you think they would risk contacting the Federation?

After all, the feds turned on them."

"That is an argument for doing nothing. But they might remain a threat and a danger to the sisters and the children," said Blanchfleur.

"And to us," said Alice. "What can we do about them?"

"No more killing," said Nora. "Not unless we absolutely have to."

"What if we went somewhere and took anyone who wants to go along with us?" said Adam.

"There's nowhere else, is there?" asked Alice. "Nowhere as safe as here."

"There are many other places," said Blanchfleur. "It's a big country."

"Not as safe as here," answered Alice. "And where are these places?"

"Maybe not. Who knows how safe we are here?" said Blanchfleur. "There are many others, you know. The Federation wants you to think there is no one outside the cities, but that's not really true when you get to remote areas. The Federation seeks out any major or successful outbreaks of illicit populations and deals with them. But the earth is too large. Small gatherings of outlaw populations and rogue communities escaped to many of the mountains and the forests.

"There is a community made up of mostly First Nations not far from here, according to Sister Thomas. They have been helpful to the convent and the convent to them. She says if we go to them, she will give us a letter of introduction and they will help us to disappear into the wild. They've done this more than once before. Their chief is named Silent Owl. She is young and sensible and very kind."

"Where will we find her?" asked Ueland.

"On the islands at the river's mouth. Her people live on the Island of the Metal Giants," said Blanchfleur.

"Metal Giants?" asked Mabon, who had been considered a giant by the old ones in the valley.

"There were once wind farms all across the island that generated electricity. They no longer function, but they still stand with their giant arms rusting," said Blanchfleur.

"Are there girls in the forest?" asked Tish.

"Yes, and many boys, too," answered her grandmother. "They may be hard to find as they stay under the cover of the trees and inside their hill houses in daylight. Sister Thomas will tell us how to meet with them. There are designated places to leave signs that are known to both of us and are checked regularly and often."

All of this information came as a shock to Tish and the others. Tish had lived her short life thinking first that Aahimsa and its domain comprised the whole world. Then she had learned that the earth was dotted with hundreds of feminine city-states and that Aahimsa was the last to contain outsider males for reproduction and as cheap labour. She knew that her grandmother had fought to keep the Manuhome functioning for its manufacturing and agricultural production. Now she suspected it was more than that, but she didn't completely get it yet. Blanchfleur had allowed the deaths of the old ones, but that was to save the Manuhome and the city. And now this information on small gatherings of "outlaw populations." She shook her head to clear it, but it didn't help.

Nora stood up. "Let's call the sisters in and try to come to some agreement. I propose that each of us consider what we will do. The choice as I understand it will be to leave here and head for this Island of the Giants with anyone who wants to go — adults, children, males, females, anyone. Those who wish to stay here will be welcomed, I'm sure. Sister Thomas tells me they have alternate housing that they can move to until they are sure there is no threat from the Federation. Mabon and I will be going outside tonight to look for signs of the traitor women. After we return, we will be leaving this lovely place along with Adam and the young sisters and their children, perhaps as early as tomorrow."

Chapter 24: Traitors

Mabon and Nora had no idea where to look for the renegade insiders who had betrayed Blanchfleur and the City of Aahimsa to the attackers from the Federation. But they were startled to discover the carelessness of their new enemies. Before coming outside they agreed that there was to be no violence and, if possible, they would merely try to locate them and determine their numbers and then leave them in peace if possible.

However, both Mabon and Nora remained keenly aware of how potentially dangerous these women could be to the sisters in the convent. And equally dangerous to all of those the sisters protected, including their own party, and to the children. Killing the traitors was the only certain way to protect everyone, but they had decided that if the world was going to ever change, the killing had to stop.

The two had grown friendly with the darkness during their years in Happy Valley with the old ones. In spite of their danger, they were enjoying the quiet time they had alone together as they climbed up to the top of the highest of the wrecked structures in the city, the bell tower of a huge stone church building on the highest hill amid the ruins of what had once been a beautiful lakeside city. More than half the church building lay in shattered wreckage. But the section housing the bell tower remained. Once Mabon had cleared away the rocks and debris from the belfry door, they found the interior with its stairs and ladders clear and intact. Standing up next to the huge bells they had a clear view of all four sides of the destroyed city and could see far out on the lake below, where it glistened here and there, reflecting the clean light of a quarter moon as far off as what they recognized as the Island of the Giants.

They moved around the belfry carefully, surveying the scenery below, watching for any movement or sign of life. They finished their first cycle without any indication of human activity catching their eye. Halfway around the second time Nora touched Mabon's right arm and pointed off to a small open area to the right.

"Is that smoke?" she said, her arm extended toward a small section of what must have been a city square. From a roofed bandstand built of grey stone, wisps of fog or perhaps smoke appeared to be rising. Soon afterward they could smell the distinct odour of burnt wood. They watched the area for what felt like a long time before they finally saw the movement they were hoping for, first one person and then another. Behind them the smoke was no longer rising.

Mabon took the stub of a pencil and a bit of paper out of his shirt pocket and began to make a rough drawing of the streets around them leading to the gazebo and from there to the convent so they could navigate their way back to the gazebo once they climbed down to street level.

"Should we get over there before they disappear?" asked Nora.

They made their way down to the main lobby of the broken church, and, as they closed the door to the belfry tower, they heard the roar of highly revved approaching engines. Nora turned to Mabon, her face showing alarm and uncertainty.

"Helicopters," he said.

"Let's go back to the convent quickly," Nora said and headed for the door.

"Wait," said Mabon. "It's not safe. Let's get back into the tower and lock the door from the inside. We're safer here and we don't want to risk being seen and giving the others away."

The racket from the motors and the whirring blades of the helicopters was deafening and there suddenly came a series of explosions from outside, blasts powerful enough that the damaged church shook violently and they feared it might completely collapse on them. Dirt, loose chunks of plaster, and bits of rotted wood rained down on them.

Several times a helicopter approached and hovered close by and then moved away. Every now and then there were explosions and bursts of rapid gunfire. Mabon wanted to climb up and look, but Nora held him back, clinging to him. She wanted them close together no matter what happened.

They clung to one another for what seemed like hours while one of the helicopters and then another landed not far away. Above the wop-wop-wop of the idling choppers they heard shots and the screams of injured and terrified victims and then silence. After another long and painful lull in the attack, the helicopters lifted once again and flew away and still they waited, unsure of their safety.

"How long should we wait?" asked Nora finally, the gold specks in her eyes visible even in the dim light that entered the middle platform of the bell tower from the full moon in the sky outside.

"They may have left one or more of their murderers behind," said Mabon. "They can't be sure how many women were out here. I think we should wait for morning. It's not a cold night. In the morning I'll check out the damage."

"*We'll* check the damage," said Nora, clinging to him.

"And both get caught?"

"Four eyes are better than two," she said, reaching up to ruffle his hair. Mabon grinned and, after a brief pause, nodded.

"Let's find a smooth bit of wall and lean back…get some sleep if we can."

"Can I lean against you?" she said. "You're a bit softer than the wall."

Mabon nodded again and she sat down against his right

side and rested her head against his broad shoulder. He wrapped an arm protectively around her and gradually her heart slowed and began to beat normally and she felt safe enough to close her eyes. Mabon struggled to relax but remained mostly restless, his mind full of the imagined horrors suffered by the former insiders from Aahimsa who had been betrayed by the city's enemies after helping them destroy their own home. No matter how fitting their punishment, it was hard for him to sit back and do nothing. But nothing was all he could do. He and Nora had too much to lose and so did all their companions if they were discovered.

Mabon awoke to early morning light that crept down the inside of the bell tower from where the bell rope hung down from the bell. The hatch at the top of the wooden ladder remained closed as they had left it. Mabon felt stiff and sore, but he was aware that moving or stretching would wake Nora. He decided he'd let her sleep as long as possible. A moment later he heard Nora sigh and felt her small hand squeeze his leg just above the knee. She turned her head and tried to smile, then looked up toward the hatch.

"Let's go have a look," she said. "But we'll have to be careful."

From the top of the tower they saw that the gazebo where they'd spotted a few of the renegade insiders no longer existed. A charred circle of broken ground had replaced it. They stood as still as statues and surveyed all they could see of the area outside, looking for any sign of movement. Nora clung tightly to Mabon. He could feel her shudder.

He, too, was horrified at all that may have happened. After several discussions, considerable anxiety, and waiting an impossibly long time during which the cool early morning dampness was replaced by midday heat, they came to a decision.

"I think it's safe to go outside and take a look around. I fear there isn't much left to see. But we can't be sure. A bit of a look around and then back to the others," said Mabon.

"Yes," said Nora. "As safe as it's ever going to be. I can't imagine how terribly worried the others will be."

Chapter 25: Adam Is Worried

It must be getting quite late, Adam thought, although he had no way of telling exactly what time it was. His parents had left shortly after everyone had eaten lunch together with the sisters. He and Tish had spent some pleasant moments exploring the greenhouses and had almost completely lost track of time when they heard explosions outside in the distance, and felt the ground shudder, and the large glass panes rattle in the starry sky above their heads. The silent workers in the huge, fragile building gathered around them and, without speaking, pointed to the door. All filed out in a long line that descended underground as swiftly as possible to the further silence and security of the convent.

That had been hours ago, and there had been no signs since of Nora and Mabon's return. How horrible it would be to lose his parents now, after they'd survived all of their adventures in the wild and in the hidden valley and all that happened after their family had been forced to separate for their own safety. And now, just after they had been joyfully reunited, to have this happen. And he didn't even know what "this" was.

But from the sound of this latest series of explosions, it had to be some part of the army of the Federation at work. They had come to complete their destruction. Somehow they must have discovered that Blanchfleur or the others from Aahimsa were here, or perhaps it was only the Aahimsa traitors they were seeking. Whatever the explanation, it couldn't be good for them. Adam tried to rest, but every time he closed his eyes he imagined that bombs were falling and cannons were blasting at his parents.

Finally he got out of his bed and made his way to the reception area with its small kitchen that was attached to the apartment allocated to Blanchfleur and her improbable party of travellers. Adam was pleasantly surprised to find the mayor sitting at a wooden table with Tish and Alice and Doctor Ueland.

"Are they back?" Adam asked hopefully. No one answered, but the adults looked from one to the other. Tish looked him in the face and shook her head. Knowing that she at least understood and sympathized with his concern about his parents' long absence helped a lot.

"What are we going to do?" Adam asked as he took a seat at a table opposite Tish.

"Nothing," said the doctor. His voice was gentle and relaxed, but he looked anxious.

"Why not?" asked Tish. "Don't you even care about them?" Her question seemed pointed toward her grandmother. All her young years, it had been the mayor who had furnished the answer to all of her questions, and now her grandmother was sitting here looking frustrated and helpless.

Blanchfleur couldn't suppress a rather nervous grin. "It's because we care about them that we are waiting. It isn't easy to wait here, not knowing what has happened outside. Once the dust settles and we are pretty sure there is no one waiting for us to appear above ground, Ueland and I will be out there looking. I'm hoping that the attack was not aimed at Nora or Mabon; the more likely target would be Gloria and that renegade insider group. But we can't be sure, and we are worried. But rushing out into the open would only prove disastrous to all of us and also to our innocent hosts. So be patient, kids, and hopefully it will all work out for the best for everyone."

Chapter 26: Trouble Overhead

"We'll have a quick, cautious look around," suggested Mabon. "One of us will move out ahead in bursts with the other watching. Then the second will join the first carefully while the first keeps watch for danger. Before we move, we pick a sheltered destination, plan the best route, and then run quickly to that destination, keeping low. Any sign of danger and the watcher will whistle like a bird once and the mover will freeze in place or hit the dirt."

"Who moves and who watches?" said Nora quietly, pushing firmly against his warm back. He leaned back to meet her pressure, enjoying the reciprocal heat of her softness, feeling empowered and comforted by her close contact.

"Let's take turns," said Mabon, turning his face and kissing the top of her head. He loved the smell of her hair. She was as much a part of him as his heart, and just as vital to his existence.

"Me first, okay?" said Nora, watching Mabon's eyes for reaction. There was none but a happy twinkle and a nervous smile.

"Sure," he agreed. "A few feet at a time and go from tree to tree, building to building, as much out of sight from all sides and from above as possible. Let's stay back from the blasted area and circle it, in case there are survivors."

"They wouldn't leave survivors, would they?" she said.

"Not on purpose. But I'll sleep better at night if we check," said Mabon, his face determined, ready for whatever they would find.

"Okay, ready… I'm going," said Nora.

Mabon embraced her and held her tight for few moments. *You never know*, he thought.

She hugged him back, aware of what he must be thinking. They had been together a long time and words were not always necessary. She said them anyway, smiling at him and holding his hands in hers. "I'll be careful," she said, and took one last look into his eyes.

They circumvented the blast site in awe and horror of the impressive destruction, its sights and its odours. No sign of the gazebo remained and on the side that was free of buildings, probably a former city park site, there were only a few of the sturdier trees still standing. There was no sign of Aahimsa's betrayers, no sign of life anywhere. They were together now, standing under a sturdy oak that had somehow managed to retain most of its leaves. Mabon shrugged and looked toward Nora. Her hazel eyes were dull; he saw no sign of the gold specks that seemed to gleam when she was filled with energy. His eyes were drawn to her forehead close to the hairline.

"Did you hurt yourself?" he asked, concerned.

"No, why do you ask?"

Mabon reached up and touched a spot on her forehead that looked to him like fresh blood. She must have bumped something as she moved from spot to spot. He showed her his red-stained finger.

"Blood," he said after sniffing it, still convinced she had injured herself in the effort to move quickly around the broken trees and shrubbery. He showed her the blood once more and waited.

She looked at it and rubbed her forehead and looked at her hand. She shrugged and Mabon checked her forehead. The spot was gone and there was no sign of injury. Instinctively, and almost as one, they looked upwards into the dense foliage of the oak tree overhead.

"I'm going up there," said Mabon, staring into the leafy branches. Without waiting for a response he scrambled up into the leafy tree, disappearing among the thick branches and the tenacious dark green leaves.

Nora waited anxiously below until she heard his exhalation of air and knew he had found something. She was unsure if she wanted to see for herself what was up there.

"She's alive, but barely," he called down to her. "But she's hurt real, real bad."

"Wait," Nora said, "I'm coming up." She climbed slowly and with great care up above the first thick branches and on to where Mabon waited next to an injured insider. She did her own deep intake of air once she recognized the face she had seen only once before, on the viewer at Alice's summer house just before Nora had fled Aahimsa and Alice carrying the baby Adam.

"What is it?", asked Mabon.

Nora didn't answer right away but finally she looked up, her hazel orbs flashing their specks of gold. "She's the worst of the Aahimsa traitors. She's the insider, the ringleader who hated Blanchfleur, the one who wanted to kill Adam and all of the outsiders. I'm almost certain this woman is Gloria, Blanchfleur's worst enemy."

"What should we do?" asked Mabon. "We could leave her here."

"That might be the best," Nora said, her voice upset and angry.

Mabon said nothing. He watched Nora's conflicted face. He could tell she wasn't finished with this. He would wait. Silently he waited, his hand against the injured insider's dirt-stained face.

"But we can't leave her here, can we?" she said finally. "What will we do?"

"We can't take her back to the convent either," said Mabon. "I think that would be dangerous and foolish. One of us should go for help and then we'll decide. We need Doctor Ueland and Sister Thomas and perhaps Blanchfleur.

They can come here and bring supplies and some food for us. We'll have Ueland check her over and then decide how we should proceed from there."

Nora set out for the convent and Mabon stayed behind with the victim of the Federation killers. He had medicines in his shoulder bag. Also in the bag was his canister of drinking water, which still contained a few drops. He and Nora had passed a small pool of rainwater that they had tasted and found acceptable. He left the woman and climbed down to fill his canteen and when he returned he found her alert enough to stare at him with absolute terror. She tried to scream and squirm up the tree away from him, but she was physically unable to do either.

"Help is on its way," he told her. He unscrewed the cap of his canteen and watched a few large drops fall between her open dry lips. In spite of her fear and trembling she accepted the water and he managed to give her a few more small sips. He opened his medicine bundle and mixed a few powders into a handful of water and got some of that concoction between her lips, too.

After a short while she seemed to relax somewhat and she closed her eyes and appeared to be asleep. Mabon watched her face and in spite of just learning the horrible things she had done, he felt very sorry for her and the suffering she would be going through if she happened to survive. Then he sat beside her in the old oak tree and waited.

Chapter 27: Gloria speaks

"What medicine did you use to treat her?" asked Blanchfleur through the door. Ueland turned, quite interested in Mabon's answer.

"A mixture of herbs and roots and dried leaves in hot water, something I learned from Brin and the old ones in Happy Valley."

Half an hour later they were called back inside the room.

Ueland pulled them aside from the injured woman, who was now awake and looking around the room. She was startled to see Blanchfleur there but the fear quickly disappeared and was replaced with curiosity and confusion.

"She has a few broken ribs, a broken collarbone, and one broken arm," said Ueland, "but I feel safe to say she has no fatal internal injuries. If she had such injuries, she'd likely already have been dead when you found her. We'll keep her undercover close to the monastery until her bones set and then we'll leave her with the sisters if they all agree. By then the insiders' troops will have stopped keeping a close watch on Queenstown."

"Can I talk with her for a moment?" asked Blanchfleur. "Is she well enough to speak with me?"

"Yes, but keep it short and simple. She needs lots of rest."

"Should we leave?" asked Mabon.

Blanchfleur shrugged. "It doesn't matter, she's your project." They stayed.

"We're glad you're going to be all right," Blanchfleur said to Gloria. Gloria nodded. She waited for more. Eventually Blanchfleur got to the point. "Do you recall how you were injured?" Gloria shook her head.

"We found you up in a huge oak tree," said Nora. "There had been a huge explosion and lots of gunfire. Do you remember it?"

Gloria shook her head again. She couldn't recall an explosion but she remembered them coming. When she spoke it was softly and with a dry throat that left her voice barely audible. "They were all around the place. I was away from the others and I was trying to hide."

"Did you know any of the people who attacked you?" asked Nora, trying to treat her with as much kindness as she could muster. She still wasn't convinced they had done the right thing by rescuing her.

Gloria turned her head quickly toward Nora. "They weren't people," said Gloria, her face reflecting the horror of the memory. "Some kind of machines that looked more like large dogs than people. Machines that could find us and then knew how to kill us all. They had no eyes, just heads that looked like revolving metal cans. They just knew how to find us. There were voices. They seemed to know all our names. I have no idea how they could recognize us without eyes. Before we saw any of them, they were calling us by name."

"You must have been terrified," said Mabon, his voice low and reassuring.

"Who are you?" she asked. Before he could answer, she said, "You were the one in the tree. You were kind to me." Gloria's voice showed that she had been confused and surprised by his kindness, especially because she expected him to hurt her more, or finish killing her.

"My name is Mabon," he answered. "Thank you. I felt bad about what they did to you. I have known much pain and suffering and I hate to see it."

"You were the cleaner," she said, suddenly recognizing him. "Great Goddess!" A tremor rocked her body and then she closed her eyes and slept.

Chapter 28: Time to Leave

The summer was drawing to a close, the air decidedly cooler and damper, as the party of travellers approached the lake. There had been little conversation since the decision had been made to leave Gloria behind with the sisters as she requested. She said that she thought she could be happy there and felt safe from further attacks from the insiders. She had met with each of the travellers and apologized to everyone, especially Blanchfleur and her family for her traitorous actions. Blanchfleur told her she was welcome to come with them on their journey to the east but Gloria said she was uncomfortable with the outsiders, even as she was grateful for their kindness and help with her injuries and her recent plight. But she wished them all well.

"I still don't get it," she had said. "We should all be enemies, but, instead, you are helping one another and acting like friends."

No one had answered. They didn't completely understand either, but somehow Blanchfleur felt understanding was highly overrated and irrelevant in this set of circumstances and probably in countless others.

And now they were all travelling together, their numbers augmented by four young women from the convent and their children, three small boys and six little girls of various ages, and were drawing near to the meeting place described by Mother Superior. Adam didn't know the children very well, but there would, with luck, be lots of time for that in the future.

Twenty minutes after crossing on the canoes and following an old paved road that led to the interior of the island, they arrived at the ruins of a large red-brick house that sat amidst an unkempt tangle of gnarled trees, grasses, and vines. A young woman wrapped in brightly coloured woven blankets sat on a hardwood rocking chair on a porch whose damaged floor tilted toward them like the stage in theatres from the distant past. She rose and waved to them as they approached. She was a tiny woman whose pretty face was tanned like brown leather and covered in blemishes, perhaps the result of chicken pox or some such disease in her childhood. But her smile was young and merry and her large dark eyes sparkled with vigour and life.

"Welcome to the maker's world, a world you may choose

to share with my people, who are willing to welcome you under certain important conditions. It is my understanding that you trust me to take all of you to a safe place where you can begin new lives together, free of persecution from your enemies. Are all of you to come with me?" The woman looked from one to the other and no one spoke. "Who is your chief? Who speaks for you?"

Blanchfleur stepped forward, along with Ueland. She spoke first. "I believe that Nora should be in charge for the time being. You can work something else out later once you become better acquainted with one another."

Nora moved up beside them, holding Mabon's hand. "Why me?" she said. "Shouldn't it be one of you?"

"I'm afraid that won't be possible," Blanchfleur said. Ueland stood close to the former mayor. He was nodding.

"Why not?" asked Nora.

"Because we have things we have to do before we return and follow you any farther to the east," said Blanchfleur.

Nora and Mabon clung to one another while Alice and Tish and Adam joined them to stand beside each of their parents. The others hung back, watching and listening. Finally Nora moved forward and addressed the young woman who was the chief among those good people who were offering their help and were generously willing to share their place of safety. "Do we have a few minutes to talk before we separate?"

The chief took a moment to answer. Then she said, "You will be their leader. There is little time to waste but I can see you need a short while to talk. Take some minutes but not long. We have only a few hours to cross the Island and paddle to the opposite shore, once known as America. We must arrive there before the coming of the first light. Come inside and have your meeting where the sky eyes cannot see us. We cannot be too careful."

They followed her down a stairway into a dark, stone-lined cellar with a hard stone floor. Down here only a trickle of moonlight crept in, barely enough to find the person ahead and to follow. Nora heard the rattle of a door handle and the creak of rusty hinges, then the young woman's clear, slow voice saying, "Wait, come in. After you shut the door, I'll light a candle."

The room was cramped and damp and the flickering candle danced like Nora's jittery nerves. Blanchfleur and Ueland moved away from the wall beside the door and approached her.

"You wanted to talk," said Blanchfleur. Ueland had his arm draped across her shoulders.

"Why aren't you coming with us?" asked Nora. "We need you. We will need all the help we can get as we adjust to life outside."

"These people will give you plenty of help. The sisters speak of them with great affection. These folks have often come to the sisters in their times of need and been happy to return the favour," said Blanchfleur. "You will be fine for a while without us around."

Everyone in the room was silent but nervous and listened attentively.

"We must leave. There are important things we have to do before we can return."

"What sort of things?" Nora asked. She was feeling

panicky. There was so much they had depended on Ueland and Blanchfleur to look after. Now all of that would fall on her and Mabon and the younger ones.

"And why have you chosen to leave together?" Adam asked. "I don't get it. You two are supposed to be enemies, aren't you?"

Blanchfleur laughed. "What makes you think that we're enemies?"

"You were on opposite sides, weren't you?" asked Mabon.

Ueland laughed as well and moved closer to Blanchfleur. "We were as close as anyone like us could get in the world we were born into," he said. "We did what we could to save the people we love."

The young chief rose and blew out the candle. "We have to go," she said, her voice firm.

"Wait." Tish's young voice broke through the darkness. "I still don't get it. How can you be standing together and leaving us all behind? Grandma, what does Ueland mean to you?"

"Ueland means everything to me, as do you and your mother," answered Blanchfleur.

"But we're family," said Alice, her tears barely visible there in the almost total darkness, her sadness clear in her breaking voice.

There was a long moment of silence before Blanchfleur spoke. "I never meant to tell you this, my darlings, but I suppose you have a right to know. Doctor Ueland is my father." There followed several intakes of breath and then a few moments of silence before Blanchfleur continued.

"My mother was a technician in the Palace of the Temple

Donors, the source of the fluids used for the temple ceremony that led to our pregnancies. She was young when she met a young donor who she was assigned to educate and train as an administrator to run the Manuhome for the mayor and her city. He was handsome and lovely and she fell in love with him. I was their child. No one ever knew the source of her pregnancy.

"She later was elected Mayor of Aahimsa and helped advance Ueland in the Manuhome and arranged his medical and scientific training. My mother trained me in politics to run for election and take over the mayoralty and I was stunned when she told me Ueland was my father. She demanded that I take care of him and work with him to preserve as many of the old ways as was possible while saving as many lives as we could. Ueland helped me build up the Manuhome from its small beginnings into the greatest industrial enterprise in the world."

"When will we see you again?" asked Tish hurriedly as people began to move to follow the young chief.

"If we can carry off our plan and survive, we'll find you again with the help of the sisters and the chief."

"What are you trying to do?" asked Mabon, leaning against Nora.

"We have to get to a reliable power source where there's a working satellite dish far enough from our friends to keep them safe from counterattack or else travel to one of the other walled cities. Obviously we'd rather find one of the systems working at one of the nearby service buildings for the rail system we came here on. They all had working satellite Internet connections before the recent attacks. I hope to find one; one is all we need.

"I have a mobile control system I removed from the Manuhome as we escaped. If all goes as I plan and no one has discovered and figured out the failsafe viruses I planted in their systems, and if we get safely through to the satellites, I can neutralize most of the military and police satellites after hacking into the systems. It's more than possible I can disable all the controls for the military aircraft, the drones, and the kill bots, those nasty little machines that made our human Rangers obsolete...that made all of us redundant. Doing that can give all of you — all of us — a fighting chance for safety and success where you're going. Where we are all hoping to go."

"Where did you get this control system?" asked Alice.

Blanchfleur and Ueland glanced at one another. He nodded; she spoke. "The Manuhome was originally given the contract by the Central Council to destroy all the old-world scientific research that could be gathered regarding past and future weapons of war. This was a move to foster a permanent global peace.

"The Council asked all of our insider cities to gather all data and materials they could uncover from their regions. In the beginning, every city was like Aahimsa in that there were walls and substantial outsider populations working and subsisting outside their walls. Outsider police and military were trained and used by controllers to keep the peace and serve the insider populations. The outsider police, mostly all trained as Rangers, gathered and shipped what they found to the Manuhome, where all was recorded and most of it destroyed. Occasionally the council decided to keep up certain lines of research.

"Industrial and military robotics was one. Once again the Manuhome was a major player in this research, development, and manufacturing. This was mostly because of Ueland's excellent use and constant education of his skilled workers. It meant years of valuable contracts for the Manuhome. Ueland was also quick to understand that these robotics, the development of industrial robots and military robotic humanoids without conscience or will, which could be completely controlled to protect the cities without ever threatening the insider population, would eventually lead to the end of all human outsiders.

"Ueland and I discussed this threat and agreed that we should keep a complete digital record of all developments and bury within all systems a fatal failsafe virus that could lie dormant in all the weapons systems, robotic and otherwise, and all weapons delivery systems, should the technology threaten us all in the future."

"Were they developed?" asked Nora.

"Yes," said Ueland. "Yes, it was my secret project. And as I was chief systems administrator and the one who designed the communication linkage systems and the command controls, I had free access to all programming details. We manufactured all those key components at the Manuhome and shipped them around the globe."

Adam had moved up next to Nora and Mabon. The big man put an arm around his shoulder. The boy spoke: "The black metal briefcase in your luggage," he said, looking Ueland in the eye. "I saw you take it from the closet on the day the Manuhome and the city were destroyed."

Ueland nodded.

"But why haven't you used the device before this? Why didn't you stop the attack?" asked Tish.

"There wasn't time," said Blanchfleur. "They took us completely by surprise and jammed all our communication systems. It would have meant an even earlier end of everything if we dared to act from Aahimsa. We and all of our equipment would have been found out and destroyed. It was better this way. Now we have a window to work in before they know we exist and where we are."

"I had to try and save as many of you as I could," said Ueland.

"But couldn't you have done something after the attack?" asked Mabon.

"There is no terminal here where I can log on to the system or recharge the device. It can only hold a charge for a limited time. All was destroyed with Aahimsa. The failsafe virus is designed to be undetectable. It doesn't exist until I activate it. It is buried in the code at thousands of points throughout all systems. Once activated it does its job and then installs elsewhere along a designated path. It is unstoppable. But I need an existing source of electric power so that I can connect with a satellite and access its data systems and get through to the central servers.

"This is where the danger lies. Once the system detects my intrusion, it will send out everything it has to destroy me and everything around me. Some of the satellites can drop armed drones from space. They have other drones that can travel very rapidly from bunkers here and there and hit with absolute accuracy any point of illicit transmission on the planet. I'm hoping to get to one of the service buildings before they're all destroyed. That is why we have to go soon. Those bots that attacked Gloria and the others with her are almost indestructible. Almost. If we can get inside the system, everything right down the line, including those bots, can be turned into a pile of worthless scrap in minutes, just like all the major storage servers and backups all across the planet."

"But what will that do to the insiders?" asked Alice.

Blanchfleur spoke: "We didn't do this before now because we wanted Adam and all of us far enough away from this device to be safe from attack. And be assured that as little harm as possible will come to the insiders. They will be free to live in peace. They just won't be able to attack one another, or us, unless they go out and do it by themselves. And they can't hurt us unless they come after us by themselves. No more attacks from space or from the sky for a long time. No helicopters, no robots — all disabled."

"What about satellite communications?" asked Mabon.

"Gone," said Ueland. "They'll have basic radio communications."

"But we'll be safe?" said Tish.

"Safe from attack by them," said Blanchfleur, "if we succeed."

"And that's far from certain," said Ueland. "But there is a real chance of success."

The chief stood and the whispering in various parts of the room gradually faded to expectant silence.

"You will be our guests in this, our land. You may see yourselves as running away from your civilization into what you see as a ruined land." She waited a moment for a reaction. Nora and Mabon and the others exchanged glances but said nothing.

"Go on, please," said Nora.

"For us, for our people, it is, in spite of the constant danger of destruction, a return of true civilization. The land has been returned to us. In many ways it has been wounded and crippled by your people and your ways, but the land has begun to heal and we are learning to live as our ancestors lived, in harmony with our world.

"So you can see that, though we are happy to share some of our land with you, we have expectations as to how you live on our land. We respect your differences and know that your people and ours will not do all things in the same manner. We can help one another and we promise to do so.

"Your presence may put us in more danger than before. We can accept that. But we cannot accept a return to the destructive and wasteful ways of the past. The plants and animals have begun to make a comeback in the forests and the streams, the birds in the skies and forests and on the land. You must learn to respect them and their homes, as we will respect yours. We can speak much more of this in the future."

Adam stood and Tish rose up from close by. Tish spoke first. "Where will we live and what will we do for food?" she asked.

"Like us, you will learn to live well. We have recently built a new village and moved from an old one. When we heard you might come, we cleaned up the old and made a few repairs. It is a fine village, close to fresh water and rich with game. Like our new village, it lies inside thick forest and is not visible from above. We will teach you how to survive without giving signs to the eyes above you."

"Can we hunt and fish?" asked Adam.

"You can take what you need of all things, but nothing more. There will be plenty for all of us. There are still few of us living here and abundance is everywhere. You will see. If we are sensible and learn to live in peace together, we will all survive. We will take you to your village soon. There is much to say, but it can wait until you are all safely at home in your village." She paused and all waited in silence. After a few nervous minutes, she continued. "Do you still want to come with us?"

"We do," said Adam.

"Yes," said Tish.

Nora nodded and there was a rush of chatter around the room and a sense of relief among the travellers.

"There is no more time!" said the chief. "It's now or never. For the next while, no talking. We will move in groups of five or six, each group staying apart from those ahead and behind. Stop every now and then and lie close together in silence. It will be the same in the canoes, where we will be as moose swimming. Until we get under the trees near the camps we are wild animals, dogs and deer and wolves. Let's go."

The young chief spoke loudly this time, with more authority. "I'm leaving now. If you want to come, follow me." She led them outside into the dark night. All followed along in silence except Ueland and Blanchfleur, who headed back toward Queenstown.

Chapter 29: Backtracking

Blanchfleur and Ueland managed to reach the outskirts of Queenstown as the darkness was being driven away by the approach of morning. The area was still shrouded in early morning fog and a light mist that was hardly perceptible as rain but nonetheless had drenched the two travellers from head to foot.

"Do you think it wise to return to the monastery this soon after leaving?" asked Blanchfleur.

"We won't be returning to the monastery," said Ueland as he stepped along in surprisingly long strides considering his short legs.

"But they have electricity," said the Blanchfleur, struggling to keep up.

"We can't expose them to any more danger," said Ueland, slowing his pace a bit and allowing her to walk next to him. Blanchfleur did what she could to keep pace with her energetic father. "The second I connect, they will have the monastery pinpointed as the point of transmission and the forces with their weapons will be on their way. I can't do that to the sisters."

"Of course, how stupid of me. Then where exactly are we going?"

"You don't have to come anywhere with me. You can wait for me here in the subway tram below, or go quietly up to the monastery if you prefer. Either option would be the preferable and much safer for you. There's no need for both of us to be at risk."

"And where will you be going, if you indeed go there on your own?" she asked.

"I plan to follow the tracks back toward Aahimsa until I find a station that hasn't been destroyed. Once I find it, I'll make sure it has the equipment I need and then try once again to fire up a generator. All the stations originally were equipped with satellite dishes that connected to the world networks. If they haven't been bombed or blasted, and my viruses have not been detected and destroyed, I will shut down all the attack capabilities of the military systems for a long time to come."

Blanchfleur was walking beside him, a bit out of breath. Ueland had been once again picking up the pace. "And if all the service buildings have been destroyed?"

"Then I will have to travel farther south to the nearest city and try to find a way to connect when I get there, a much more difficult scenario."

"I'm going with you. I can't stand the thought of keeping still, not knowing where you are or if you're living or dead, successful or beaten. What would I do with my time?"

"Once I do connect, they could destroy us very quickly. I don't want you to die," he said. "Not after we've come this far."

"What are our chances of success?" she said, grabbing at his right arm and slowing him down.

He stopped and set down his case, then sat on the wet surface of a large boulder just off the side of the trail they had been following. The day was becoming brighter and from where they were stopped, in the near distance the station building and the entrance to the Queenstown underground were emerging from the mist and the fog.

"Our chances depend on how vigilant the controllers are at the moment when we connect. I'll have to power up the generator and connect my computer to check the signal strength. If we can do all that without detection, it only takes a moment or two to release the destruct command. A few minutes later, it could be all over. If it's a clear night we may be able to watch the results as the satellites crash and die, as we make a run for it. And if we're lucky, we may be able to re-join the others." Ueland stood. "It's up to you. You have to decide if you're coming with me or staying behind."

Ueland wanted someone along for company. His had been a lonely life and he preferred not to die a lonely death, but he felt it would be selfish and stupid to insist she come along with him.

"I'm going," she said. "I want to be part of this. It's the least I can do."

A short time later they had descended into the underground tunnel and were surprised to discover the glow of some modest light source visible through the windshield of the engine that had carried them and their fellow travellers on the last part of their journey to Queenstown. Ueland signalled for Blanchfleur to remain silent. Her eyes told him all he needed to know about the questions forming in her mind, the same ones that occurred to him.

They were unarmed and had no intention of risking their mission in senseless bravado. But in spite of their best caution they both tripped over something that set a string of tin cans to rattling. The light inside the cabin of the train's engine car went out and left all in complete darkness.

"Stay here," whispered Blanchfleur and she stepped suddenly toward the car. "Don't move." There was silence in the dark tunnel for a long few minutes and then the sound of a feminine voice whimpering, then footsteps descending metal stairs. Ueland waited. A match was struck and its meagre light seemed startlingly brilliant at first. Blanchfleur's face appeared, and then her body, followed by the trembling figure of Gloria, the traitor.

"What are you doing here?" asked Ueland, his voice sharp and angry. "Shouldn't you be at the monastery with the sisters? Didn't you decide to stay back with them?"

Blanchfleur said nothing; she waited for an answer from

Gloria. She could feel the bile rising into her throat and souring her mouth. This was all they needed.

"I can't stay here. I'd rather die," she said, her voice child-like and petulant.

"You may get your wish," Ueland said. "You would be much, much safer inside, if only for the time being."

"What are you two doing here? Are you planning to go somewhere?" said Gloria. She had stopped the whimpering and now her voice sounded excited with new possibilities. Both Blanchfleur and Ueland found her behaviour annoying. How could they trust someone whose emotions were so shallow and manipulative?

"There is something we need to do. It is a very important and highly dangerous undertaking," said Blanchfleur.

Gloria's eyes glistened with tears and some sign of hope after Blanchfleur struck a second wooden match. "Can I go with you?"

Blanchfleur looked at her, saw that she was serious, and glanced at Ueland. "Don't be ridiculous," she said. "This is risky enough without you hanging on to us."

Ueland looked at Blanchfleur and shrugged. "Let's get moving. There's no time to waste arguing. Follow me... and no more matches." He turned to Blanchfleur and said quietly, "It is probably better to have her with us where we can see her than to be worrying what she might be up to when we're gone."

The threesome left the tunnel and made their way downhill toward the wooded area that separated them from the river. They wanted to travel by daylight and as quickly as possible, and needed the protection of the treetops overhead to separate them from the eyes in space.

Late in their third afternoon, they arrived in the vicinity of a service building that appeared, from where they stood on the fringe of the wood, to be completely intact. Several hours before, they had passed the rubble of another structure that had been recently destroyed. Ueland and Blanchfleur agreed with Gloria that it had likely been bombed by the same robotic raiders who had almost killed her and had wiped out all of her companions.

The outside air under the trees was refreshing but damp and cool, and all were looking forward to the security and shelter of the building. Thus they arrived safely and were much relieved when Ueland used his keys and let them inside the aboveground structure. It was decided that they would not try to start the generators until it was dark and they had had some rest. Gloria was warned not to touch anything or do anything that could be detected from overhead, nor to risk going outside. She was assured that if all went well they and all the others they had left behind would be guaranteed a degree of safety from attack by the cities, at least for the time being. And perhaps even for years to come.

Once inside, Ueland explained to Gloria how he had been involved in the design, construction, and maintenance of the subway line and the service buildings. Blanchfleur opened the interior door into the sleeping quarters with its bunk beds. She stepped into the windowless room and, after her eyes adjusted to the near darkness, she inspected the beds, all of which were covered by sheets of clear plastic, made up neatly, and apart from a bit of dust that had settled on them, were ready to be slept in. Soon they were all sound asleep.

Blanchfleur woke first and found herself in total blackness. After she paused long enough to recall where she was, her eyes adjusted and she could make out the faint outline of the open door of the room. She got out of her bed and moved quietly so as to not disturb Ueland, who was in the top bunk above her, or Gloria, in the lower bunk across the room beyond the kitchen counter between the beds.

Blanchfleur went out the door and entered the large exterior room. The moon and stars outside provided a surprising amount of light through the high windows above a long couch close to the door where they had entered the building. She was tempted to try and activate the generator but figured there was good reason to wait for Ueland. He had built all of this system while carrying out the upgrade to the old tourist subway. It had been her request, her idea. Yet he had been in complete charge of the details.

That was how they always worked, and he had never let her down. In that way he had been a faithful father, the best he could be under the circumstances. The backup batteries would probably be weak by now, or dead. There was a way to charge them — she remembered that, but again, not the details. She would wait until the others woke up. She moved to the sofa and lay down. She fell asleep.

She was wakened by the interior door opening with the faint sound of dry metal scraping together. The hinges needed an oiling. She could hear a small engine running somewhere outside the door. As expected, Doctor Ueland stepped inside, closing the door slowly. Blanchfleur smiled, knowing he was trying not to make noise, but the slow movement only managed to prolong the squealing of the hinges.

"Good morning," she said, smiling at Ueland.

"I am charging the starter batteries with the small gas-powered generator. We can start the large generator in about an hour," Ueland said.

"I thought so. Did you get any sleep?" she said.

"Sufficient. I'm feeling just fine. How about yourself? You chose to sleep on the couch?"

"Yes, the old sofa was quite comfortable."

The bedroom door opened wide and Gloria stepped out into the room. She turned toward the exterior door.

"You're not going outside, are you?" asked Blanchfleur.

"Yes, I am. I have to go and the toilet has no water."

"There'll be plenty of water in less than an hour after I fire up the generators," said Ueland, his voice impatient.

"I can't wait," said Gloria. It annoyed her that this outsider thought he was in charge of her. She started toward the exterior door.

"Use the toilet," said Blanchfleur quite firmly.

"I'd rather not," said Gloria, her voice whiney and defiant.

"Then you have to hold on," said Blanchfleur. "There's just no choice. You wanted to come with us and now you have to follow our rules for your own and for our safety. You of all people should know how dangerous these attackers can be."

"I'll just be a few minutes," the younger woman insisted.

"Besides, there are no attackers here now. It won't hurt to go out for a couple of minutes."

Ueland moved to block the door. "No one goes outside. The day is coming on and we can't risk being spotted until we power up. Please use the toilet just off the bedroom. Go in the door, straight ahead; the door to the left of the sink."

Gloria moved toward Ueland, as if to defy him. Blanchfleur rushed to Ueland's side. Gloria hesitated, then turned and entered the bedroom. "I know where the toilet is. I just don't want to use it without water." The once powerful mayor and her elderly father looked at one another, shrugged, and sighed.

"Can you stay here and watch the door? I'm going down to check the battery charge level. I'll be up in a while to start the big generator. My laptop should be pretty much charged by now. With a bit of luck we can do this from here. Don't let that determined little brat outside. She could ruin everything."

"I'll watch her, Doctor," said Blanchfleur with a yawn. She was still tired out. It had been more walking than she was accustomed to doing.

"You have to admire her persistence," said Ueland as diplomatically as possible.

"Yes, or her complete insanity. She has almost gotten herself murdered, and she got her cohort slaughtered. She could kill herself yet. Not to mention all of the rest of us."

"There is that," said Ueland with a chuckle as he shrugged and exited to the tunnel below.

Chapter 30: The Deserted Village by the Lake

It was dark now in their secluded village, and the travellers were settled in their sleeping rolls and blankets, most of which had been supplied by the sisters back at the monastery. The people who had led them to the village had left for the night after showing them around the various sleeping shelters, a combination of teepees and other structures with debarked poles fastened together at the top and covered with layers of birch bark and old and hardened animal furs, and bits and pieces of metal and wood and plastic.

Inside of each shelter there lingered a strong odour of old campfires that had left the interior walls blackened with soot, especially where the tops of the poles were tied together. But the travellers were tired and comfortably out of the chilly, damp wind. Most of the children were now deeply asleep and the sound of their breathing, rather than an annoyance, had become a comfort.

Adam and Tish lay wrapped in their wool blankets and animal furs on opposite sides of the tall tent. Neither was yet asleep. Adam had been gazing up at the vent overhead, probably designed to let out smoke from the fires. The visible sky was studded with stars and, despite the uncertain future, he felt surprisingly happy. He and the mayor's granddaughter had been placed in charge of the youngsters from the monastery and he felt very grown-up. He hoped nothing happened where he would have to protect them all, because he had no idea how he would manage that. Tish's voice interrupted his drowsy thoughts.

"Are you asleep?" she asked in her small sweet voice.

"No," he said. He thought of asking her the same question but caught himself in time. They had become friends, but he still wasn't used to talking to a young kid like himself and especially to an insider kid — a girl.

Mabon and Nora lay side by side under another pile of heavy blankets and furs in a second, smaller structure several steps from the children's tent. This shelter was also circular at the base and was constructed of spruce saplings tied and woven together, but unlike the children's teepee, or the third where the adults from the monastery were to sleep for now, it was not conical, but rather rounded at the top, the opening above the fire pit a neat circle. They were alone in their wigwam tonight and feeling happy to have arrived here safely. It began as a warm night, but there was now just a hint of the cooling that would bring the autumn and eventually the freezing cold of winter. Nora, after looking upward and commenting on the stars overhead, had lapsed into silence.

Mabon watched her beloved face in the beam of light that entered the teepee through the overhead opening as projected by the moon, which was not visible in the small portion of sky available to him up above.

"What are you thinking?" he whispered.

"About Ueland and Blanchfleur," she said, yawning. "Will we ever see them again?"

"I hope so," he said, turning to her. He raised himself up on one elbow. He could smell the spruce boughs that helped to soften the hardened ground under them.

"They are putting themselves into great danger for all of us, aren't they?" She reached over, took hold of his arm, and squeezed it lightly. She felt comforted by his nearness and the inherent strength of his relaxed sinews and muscles.

"Yes," he said, enjoying the softness and warmth of her grip. He remembered how lonely his life had been long ago, without her. He looked at her silhouette and felt a wave of pleasure and joy fill his giant frame.

"And even if they do manage to do what they have set out to do, they might be found and killed. Who would have dreamed it possible for Blanchfleur to be our ally and protector?"

"I hope they are not killed," said Mabon. "Yes, it is so hard to judge the actions of others when we don't know their lives. I don't even understand us. The world changes and we change with it, don't we?"

"And they might not be able to find us if they do survive," said Nora. "It's all so crazy."

Mabon shuffled his large frame across the soft furs and took her in his arms. She moved easily against him, both feeling their familiar combined warmth flood them with their now accustomed magic. Neither spoke at first, but sighed and released their tensed breaths. Mabon spoke then.

"They will find us," he said, his lips against her ear, his voice soft and reassuring. "They will come home to us no matter what happens."

"Are you sure?" she said, her confidence growing with his every word, his every breath.

"I would bet my life on it," he said just before she silenced him with kisses.

Chapter 31: Gloria Leaves the Service Building

Blanchfleur woke and felt something was amiss. She could hear nothing and see nothing in the complete darkness of the room other than the hum of the large generator below them and the soft patter of heavy rain falling outside. Ueland must have gone down below after starting the generator. She rose from the sofa and stood up on the firm cushion and gazed out into the blackness. She thought she picked up some indefinable movement in the gloomy distance but couldn't be sure.

She stepped down to the floor and walked to the door that led to the rumbling generator below. She tried the knob but the door was locked. She crossed the room carefully, looking for the door to the sleeping quarters and found it after a brief and gentle collision with the left end of the control console.

She opened the door, felt around for the light switch for the overhead light in the windowless room, and, although she hated the thought of waking her, she had to know if Gloria was, indeed, gone. She closed the door, took a deep breath and closed her eyes, then flicked the switch. She opened them and looked around.

Gloria's bed was empty. Ueland had awoken and was drowsily looking at her. She had been wrong about him. He hadn't been below. He had been sleeping soundly in one of the bunks. The washroom — perhaps she was in the washroom. She crossed the room and tapped gently, and then opened the door. The small room was empty. No one had used the toilet. She checked the corridor to the back door. No one. Gloria had to be outside.

"Are you awake, Ueland?" she called loudly from the door of the bathroom.

He jumped up instantly, startled by the panic in her voice. "What is it, Blanchfleur?" he asked. "Is something the matter?"

"Gloria is outside," she said. "I fell asleep. Sorry."

"Are you sure she's outside?" he asked. "Of course you are." He looked around at the empty bunks, the open bathroom door.

"Sorry," said Blanchfleur.

"Can you go look for her? I'll go below and try to contact one of the satellites. Find her and bring her back if you can."

"It's so dark and pouring rain, but I'll try."

"Give me a few minutes and if she's gone, get back here as fast as you can."

"Okay," said Blanchfleur. She felt disappointment; she wanted to watch as Ueland tried to contact the satellite and shut down all the operating systems. But she found a jacket and hurried outside into the darkness and the pounding rain.

Ueland opened the titanium case and removed the computer. He would get up close to the highest of the windows and begin. He set the machine on the windowsill as Blanchfleur disappeared into the darkness. That was when she heard the roar of a large engine overhead and soon she heard Gloria's scream as the lights flashing down beside the trees below her indicated that a huge battle copter had landed. She tried to control her panic as she tore through the downpour headed for the terrified Gloria.

A few minutes later she found her former enemy standing, crying in despair, surrounded by a dozen silly-looking bots. They looked like small metal horses or large dogs. They had four metal legs and a metal body shaped like a deer's and a head that spun like a big tin can. On their backs they carried small rocket-like things and a mini cannon of some sort. Blanchfleur watched as two pairs of them broke away from the circle and, prancing about like horses on their springy legs, they quickly ran in giddy circles around her and herded her back inside the large ring of these creatures until she stood next to Gloria. Gloria wrapped her arms around Blanchfleur and held her tight like she was a frightened child.

Watching these robots dance and swing around them almost made Blanchfleur laugh because in a way they looked like a friendly herd of deer, but their constantly rotating eyeless heads reminded her that these were not animals, good or evil; they had no eyes, though they saw everything, and they had no hearts or souls either. They did what they were told, without conscience, without regret, then they returned to their lairs where they silently awaited their next command.

A heavy clap of thunder and an accompanying brilliant bolt of lightning startled Ueland as he worked frantically at the computer. He glanced out the window at precisely the best moment to see the two insiders, his daughter and their common enemy, now both reduced to helpless prisoners being herded inside the copter. His heart sank but he returned to the work he had no choice but to continue. And he could not fail. He must succeed.

Inside the chopper, Blanchfleur held Gloria close to her as the robots hopped aboard and moved to slots along the walls, where most of them folded up like jackknives and fitted inside. The rotor overhead increased its revolutions as the engine roared louder and the copter began to lift off the ground, but then, almost immediately, the engine slowed, the rotor gradually stopped, and the copter settled back to the ground.

The doors opened and the bots jumped out, leaving one of their number between the prisoners and the door as a guard. Through the windows of the copter, Blanchfleur watched as the pack of robots scampered up the hill toward the service building, toward Ueland and his computer.

"Great Goddess!" Blanchfleur yelled, and the guard robot pranced toward her. At the same moment, Gloria sprang from the mayor's arms and threw her entire weight against the startled machine. Blanchfleur added her strength and the robot fell out of the machine and onto the ground. Blanchfleur slammed and locked the big door and the robot looked up at them, obviously confused, as it knew it mustn't fire on its only way to return to base. In the distance the kill bots were firing at the service centre and there were loud explosions. The robot outside the copter decided it should join the pack and it bolted up toward the others.

Gloria was over by the control panel and Blanchfleur joined her. "The panel looks the same or similar to the panel on the train we came up on, doesn't it? I wonder," the mayor said. "Do you think it has auto pilot? It must, it carries robots." She pushed the button that said, "Start" and the engine started up. She pushed the button that was marked with a "U" and the copter rose up in the air and hovered about thirty metres in the air.

Gloria was watching the attack on the service building as another explosion blasted part of a wall from the building.

"They must have seen us and were afraid they were being left behind. Do you think they can be afraid? They've stopped firing," she said. "They're coming back."

Chapter 32: Attack on the Camp

Tish heard it first: the distant roar of large aircraft and the far-off rattle of several guns. *Some of the forest people must be under attack*, she thought. She rose and woke Adam, who had finally dropped off to sleep. Together they walked outside.

"They must be attacking the new village the people spoke of," Adam said once they were outside.

"Should we wake the others?" she asked.

He took her hand. They stood like that for a while and

Adam said, "It's better to let them sleep. If they know where we are we'll be next. Let's stay silent and still and hope they don't know we're here."

"Should we try and help the people who helped us?" she said.

"I wish there was a way," Adam said. "If they come closer we'll wake everyone and try to hide. I expect the people know best how to get away in this place."

They sat under the trees and watched the sky as scattered gunfire continued in the distance.

"Look!" said Tish, "The sky...what's happening in the sky? Are those shooting stars?"

"I'm not sure," said Adam. "There are too many of them to be stars. Quick, let's wake the others."

As the others ran from their shelters, the distant gunfire stopped suddenly and the shooting stars began to fall like rain, all across the sky.

There were many cries, first of confusion and frustration at being awakened from various stages of sleep, and then turning to wonder and astonishment. They'd formed small groups of individuals familiar to one another and then into a common mass of bodies staring up and pointing at the brilliant overhead display.

Nora and Mabon were standing on one side of Adam and Tish, Alice close on the other side.

"They've done it," said Nora, her voice excited and almost shouting. "They've really done it, haven't they?"

"Do you think they'll get back safely to us?" asked Adam.

"They better," said Alice. "We can't get along without them."

"Will we be safe now?" Tish whispered to Adam, who was close beside her.

Adam paused and wondered what the right answer was. He wanted to encourage her but didn't want to lie.

"It looks good. It looks like Ueland did what he said he would do. If those are satellites and war machines falling from the sky, there will be fewer attacks from the Federation and maybe no more attacks, at least until they figure out how to get more satellites up there. But we will still have to work hard to learn how to live out here in this wild place."

"Let's celebrate this night and start to work on tomorrow in the morning," said Mabon. "We'll enjoy the light show and then get back to sleep. Listen...can you hear anything? Can you hear guns and explosions? Can you hear copters or kill bots?" He paused and everyone stopped their chatter.

"I can hear something beautiful," said Tish. "I can hear nothing but nothing."

"Silence; there is silence all around us," said Nora. "Let's sleep happily tonight."

Chapter 33: Visitors

Late in the afternoon of the sixth day after the one that ended with what everyone called "the night the stars fell" for years afterwards, two visitors arrived from the new village up the river from where Nora and her group were looking over the food and the implements their hosts had left for them. One of them was the chief who had led them here.

Nora's group waited shyly until the twosome closely approached where they had been sitting beside a pile of metal traps, pots and pans, snowshoes made of bent wood and sinews, bows and arrows of maple and poplar, spears with stone and metal points, and many other things.

"We have come to teach you of our old ways," said the chief. "This is my son, Lone Cloud. He will teach you how to hunt, trap, and gather food from the forest and the water. He will teach you to build and repair wigwams. I will teach you how to prepare clothing and bedding from animal skins, how to clean and cook the food that is brought to you, and everything else you want to know. I will teach you how to meet all of your needs without damaging the places where you will live. You will be like us, a part of this place, and we will live in peace and harmony."

Later that evening they were preparing the fires for night when a dirty and almost unrecognizable person stumbled into the tent that Adam and Tish were to share with the other children and Lone Cloud, and she fell to the dirt floor. She was followed by another young man, who entered and stood silently above her.

"Who is this, Paul, and where did you get her?" said Lone Cloud. "No one is to be brought here without consulting our mother."

"She was injured and has burns. She knew about all of you and said she was with you earlier. She was able to describe Mother and what she was wearing when she met you on the island at the head of the river. I knew it was safe, brother."

Adam and Tish followed Lone Cloud as he approached the woman on the floor. Tish looked closely at her and cried out, "Her hair and face have been burned. Oh Great

Goddess, it's my grandmother!"

"I'll get Nora, Mabon, and the chief," said Adam. "Thank you, Paul, for bringing her to us."

"Where did you find my grandmother?" asked Tish. She was on her knees up close to Blanchfleur. She was content to see that she appeared to be breathing normally.

Paul was standing beside his brother, Lone Cloud. They had been speaking quietly in the background. Paul was thin and very tall. The light in the sleeping wigwam was dim and it wasn't possible to see the colour of his eyes, but they were large and focused on the young girl beside the older woman.

"This woman appeared at the house on the island. We spoke and we talked. I agreed to take her across the water last night. We travelled slowly today. Her collarbone is broken on the right and probably some of her ribs. She has bad bruises all over that side, too. Most of her injuries happened when a chopper motor stopped in mid-air and it crashed. She got the burns trying to rescue someone from a fire. I'm still mixed up. I think someone with her died on the copter, but I don't know what happened in the fire."

Several hours later, well past bedtime, after Blanchfleur was washed and treated by Nora and the chief using some of Mabon's medicine for discomfort and his salve for the burns, everyone in Nora's group, along with the chief and two of her sons, were gathered around Blanchfleur. She was awake and as comfortable as she could be. They were in Nora and Mabon's wigwam, where Blanchfleur would be sleeping for the time being, and where she had asked to speak to everyone.

Once they were all accounted for, except the smallest of the children, Blanchfleur told them about finding Gloria hiding on the train in the tunnel and how she insisted on coming along. She had been a nuisance most of the time and had nearly inadvertently ruined their mission and led to their deaths to boot.

"But in the end," said Blanchfleur, "she saved my life — probably all of our lives. She and I had been captured and trapped by a herd of four-legged robot animals which actually herded us into their helicopter and went to attack the service building where Ueland was trying to contact the servers to unleash his killer virus against the entire Federation's military and mass communications systems. There was one of these killer robots guarding us and Gloria caught it off guard and, with a bit of help from me, pushed it out the door."

"What happened then?" asked Tish, her eyes bright. Adam watched her closely, glad she was asking the question that was on all their minds.

"Gloria and I figured out how to get the copter started and airborne," she said, her voice tired.

"Did you crash it?" asked Tish.

"No," said Blanchfleur, "the chopper fell when everything stopped. It must have been Ueland's failsafe virus, because everything stopped working at the same time, all of the robots and the helicopter, too. I didn't know about the robots stopping until later, though. All I knew was that the motors in the chopper stopped and the lights dimmed to emergency battery setting and then we hit the ground. I was unconscious for a while and when I woke up and got my brain going I could feel the pain. It took me a while to untangle myself from the debris around me. I was confused and frightened, thinking the robots had shot us down.

"Then I found Gloria. She must have hit her head hard, because it had been bleeding profusely and she was completely still. I couldn't find a heartbeat and she was no longer breathing. I looked outside and there was still barely enough light to see the robots curled up in the jackknife position all over the space in front of the service building, which was smoldering and burning as I watched. It took me a while to exit the copter and to make my way up the hill."

"Did you find your father?" asked Adam, his voice cautious and concerned. "Is Doctor Ueland okay?"

"I got inside the ruins, passing fire and heat and broken glass and fractured metal and wood. My father was pinned under a great pile of rubble, but he was alive. I told him his virus had worked and that he had probably saved everyone and how Gloria had been a hero like him. I told him I loved him. He asked if I was hurt and I said I was okay. He was very weak and was afraid that I would die in there. He told me my hair had been burned and that my skin was very red.

"I spotted the computer and its case on the floor outside the heap of debris that held him. I stayed and held his hand until he was gone. Just before that he looked into my eyes and said he loved me, too, and that he was proud of me."

"Did you leave the case behind?" asked Mabon.

"I took it and hid it in one of the ventilation ducts in

the tunnel. I hope no one ever finds it. We need to make a better, kinder world for all of us, for everyone everywhere. Once I got out of there, I started for home." She paused. "I need to sleep now. You should go to bed."

EPILOGUE

"Do you really think we can make a better world?" asked Tish when they were back in their wigwam. The others were asleep, the older ones snoring in chorus.

"I don't know," answered Adam. "I grew up in a better place than this; at least I knew how to live there. This is all so new and scary."

"The same for me. I liked Aahimsa. Life was nice there," said Tish.

"Yes, but I want to live where nobody has to kill anyone on purpose," said Adam.

"Do you think that's possible?" asked Tish, yawning and nearly asleep.

"I don't know," said Adam. "But I'm going to try. Goodnight, Tish."

"Me, too… I'd like that. I'd really like that. Goodnight, Adam."

He looked up at the opening at the top of their tepee. The satellites were no longer falling and there were only stars shining brightly overhead. He looked over at Tish, who was now asleep. Her face was as peaceful as the starry sky. *I'd really like that, too*, he thought. He felt warm inside and realized he didn't feel scared anymore, just cozy and tired. He felt like he was home again in the Happy Valley, and he couldn't wait for tomorrow.

Acknowledgements

I would like to thank the uncountable many who have inspired my love of reading and writing: parents, teachers, librarians, editors, publishers, book sellers and the written legacy of those who worked to make the world known, and the decency, peace and justice sought-after through their writing.